I0641291

# A Romanorum Anthology

**Legends of the Romanorum, Volume 3.6**

Mychael Black and Shayne Carmichael

Published by Arian Derwydd Books, LLC, 2024.

# Table of Contents

*Legends of the Romanorum, 3-6*
# AUTHORS' NOTE:

All stories in this anthology are part of the Legends of the Romanorum series. They are in order, from #3 to #6. Book #7, *Forever May Not Be Long Enough*, takes place after this anthology in terms of timeline.

**Beneath the Mask (#3), chapters 1-12**: Lance Shaw has secured an interview with the leader of the Inferi Brotherhood, a group of vampires that broke off from the Romanorum in the 13th century. Triarius is petite but possesses a personality that far exceeds anyone Lance has ever known. Triarius isn't beautiful by any means, and the silver mask he wears over half his scarred face attests to the brutality of his world.

**Sight Unseen (#4), chapters 13-20**: Jamie Smith runs an antique shop, and he thinks Samuel Haridan might be the most interesting customer he's ever had. Haridan is looking for a pearl necklace, but before he and Jamie can even start to negotiate, they're interrupted by a break-in. Jamie enters a whole new world, and just as he and Haridan begin to explore their chemistry, a kidnapping forces them apart.

**Necessary Evil (#5), chapters 21-27**: Life with Triarius is anything but dull. When Triarius tells him about a vampiric son named Aldrich, Lance isn't sure what to think. To make matters worse, Lance finds himself drawn to Triarius' general, Apollonius. Can Lance, Triarius, and Apollonius keep their people safe? Or will an announcement from Triarius seal their fates once and for all?

**Dreams of Death (#6), chapters 28-33**: A new serial killer is on the loose. As the bodies pile up, the police scrambled to make sense of the bizarre pieces of evidence. A gang of hackers following the case know the killer isn't human, and they're putting the clues together faster than the police can. Aaron tracks down the vampire, not about to let fear or sanity stand in his way.

This book is a work of fiction. Any resemblance to persons, living or dead, actual events, locale, or organizations is entirely coincidental.

Arian Derwydd Books, LLC

https://arianderwyddbooks.com/

A Romanorum Anthology

Copyright © 2024 by Shayne Carmichael & Mychael Black

ISBN: 979-8-9902245-5-1

*Legends of the Romanorum, Book 3*
Beneath the Mask

# Chapter One

"Thank you for meeting me like this."

"My pleasure."

I flipped open my notebook to a fresh page and tried to ignore the slight shakiness in my hand as I clicked my pen. "I'm just going to jot down some initial notes. If anything is wrong, please feel free to correct me." There was no answer, but when I glanced up, I saw the shadowed figure nod. I fixed my gaze back onto my paper. "Triarius... Any last name?"

"No."

I continued. "Born in Rome in 12 BC, turned in 7 AD." I paused. "You're... over two thousand years old?"

"I am."

I stifled a sigh. Maybe this was a mistake. When Jeff gave me this lead, I had high hopes of a great interview—the pinnacle of my career. Yes, vampires were quite well-known to exist, and some even held ranks within the human government, but aside from a few instances, getting into their circle was next to impossible. And that was just the Romanorum. This... was the Brotherhood. I twirled my pen in my fingers, wondering just how to start this. I've been interviewing vampires for nearly fifteen years. Why was this one so different?

"Is there something wrong, Mr. Shaw?"

"No!" I shook my head. "No, no." I cleared my throat. "I asked you here to fulfill an opportunity—for us both. A chance for me to, quite honestly, get the story of the century: the history of the Inferi Brotherhood. And a chance for you to dispel the rumors of... well... less than pleasant acts said to occur within the Brotherhood."

"And what if the rumors are true?"

I swallowed compulsively, my mouth and throat suddenly dry. "True?" He stood and I watched him walk over to the window. Moonlight shone through the glass around his body. He was shorter than I'd expected, for some reason, and of slighter build. I'd thought one of the most feared men in the world would be much larger in stature.

"Size matters little when compared to the mind, Mr. Shaw," he said without turning. He clasped his hands behind his back, shoulders straight and squared. On a lesser man, the position might have been seen as bravado; on him, it seemed natural. "I created the Brotherhood because I no longer felt the Romanorum served its purpose."

"What if Diocourides were to find out? He would-"

"Dio knows we exist, Mr. Shaw. The Romanorum knows. At this point, I would daresay the entire world knows. The fact remains, however, that they cannot find the worst of us. And by that, I mean those of us who actively kill humans."

Fuck. I was in over my head. What was I thinking? Here I was, in some nondescript ghost town in the middle of nowhere England, with a man—a creature—who could easily kill me. And no one would ever know. Curiosity, however, is a strong influence.

"I know the Brotherhood is underground—both figuratively and literally, and no, I won't ask where. I am curious, though, as to why the Romanorum can't find you. Can't every vampire—even a rogue—trace his or her blood back to the sire?"

"Not all of us are rogues," he said. "It is true that I myself am, by Romanorum standards, but you forget that the oldest of us did not take the formulas required to make that distinction. It is by name alone that I am known for who I am, not by any taint to my aura or soul."

"So... there are those who are not rogues within the Brotherhood?"

"Yes. The Brotherhood is not based on killing humans. We are gods, Mr. Shaw. Descended from gods, created by them. Human are cattle, put upon this earth for us to use as we see fit."

"The Romanorum would have something to say about that," I said quietly.

"You are not writing. Is my tale that uninteresting?"

I blinked down at the paper. A large stain spread out from where the tip of my pen rested, but there were no words. What was I supposed to say, how was I going to write any of this into a news story? I stared at the blotch of ink and wondered why I'd even asked for this meeting.

"Perhaps you were curious, more for your own sake than that of your readers."

"You can read minds."

"I can."

I figured the best step would be to find out more about the man behind it all. "What else can you do?"

Triarius chuckled, still facing away from me. "Much. More than you could ever begin to explain to your readers, Mr. Shaw."

It occurred to me then that I had no idea what this man even looked like. He was here when I'd arrived, cloaked in shadows. "What do you look like?"

"Another question for your story?"

"No." For me...

Triarius turned and my heart nearly stopped. Light glinted off of something silver on the right side of his face. Like some real-life twist on the Phantom, Triarius had a silver mask—or at least half of one—covering the upper right side of his face. There was a hole for him to see out of, and the mask stopped just an inch or so above his mouth, and then tapered off to the side. The eye peering through the hole in the mask was milky white, almost glassy. His other was steel blue. His lips curled into a twisted smile that said he knew exactly what I was thinking.

"I was disfigured long before my turning. A bit of sparring gone wrong, you could say."

I could tell there was more to it, but he didn't seem inclined to elaborate. He stepped away from the window and closer to the table where I sat. The shadows seemed to move with him, somehow, wrapping around his body like a cloak. I knew some vampires were able to control the shadows. I'd even been witness to the Prince of London toying with them a time or two. These shadows were much different, though—thicker, consuming.

Like Triarius, they seemed to draw in the light, engulfing it until there was nothing left. I wanted to say this man was evil, but even that felt inadequate for what I saw in his eyes. There was power behind them, more than I think anyone ever realized, but there was something darker. I knew he was a rogue—he'd said so himself. This went beyond being a rogue. It wasn't blood lust that fueled him. It was the worst kind of power imaginable: unspoken, quiet, calculating.

Triarius settled back into his seat and the darkness enveloped him. His unassuming voice broke the awkward silence. "I created the Brotherhood in 1232. To this date, there are thousands of us, spread throughout the world. We have a network, a system through which we conduct business, recruit, and if need be, dispose of unwanted influences."

"Unwanted influences?"

"Every organization has its share of bad seeds. We deal with ours effectively—within and without the Brotherhood itself."

"So you are murderers, killing without the need to drink, then."

Triarius clicked his tongue, the sound loud in the small room. "Come now, Mr. Shaw. Murder is such a strong word, don't you think? I prefer... cleansing."

"How do you do it?"

"We receive reports, from our members out in the open. We then send teams to investigate. If we find the reports to be true, the subjects in question to be threats, then we dispose of them—quickly and efficiently. If an answer cannot be determined right away, the subjects are brought to me."

I felt the blood slowly drain from my face and I shivered as the temperature in the room dropped several degrees. "And you hold them prisoner? How do you determine if they are a threat or not?"

"There are many ways to prompt a person to speak when he or she is not normally inclined to do so."

"Torture?"

"If necessary, though I find it tedious. I prefer mind over body. The mind does not lie, only the mouth. If I want truth, I need only to see a person's thoughts."

"So you invade their brains, basically?"

"My, but you are abrasive in your choice of words." He sighed. "But yes, I do."

"I guess it's pointless to argue about morals, then."

Triarius laughed. "Mr. Shaw, I have, in my two thousand years, taken great pleasure in watching men die. Do you really think morals matter to me?"

"No." I had to look away. Something in his stare unhinged me. I didn't like feeling as if I was a bug under a microscope, and yet, despite being the interviewer, that's precisely what I felt like. "So..." My brain frantically searched for something else to say, something to ask him. Anything to keep the conversation going. "Is there anything else you'd like to tell me about the Brotherhood?"

"Aside from where we are, details of our membership, all of which would require me to kill you lest it get out? No."

I blew out a breath. "Okay," I announced. "I think I have enough to write up a good piece here." I closed my notebook, tucked the pen in the spiral, and stood. "I want to thank you for this opportunity, Triarius. I'm sure my readers will find it very interesting." I started for the door, only to have it close before I reached it.

"I am afraid you are mistaken, Mr. Shaw." He hadn't moved. "I cannot allow you to publish anything I've told you."

"Excuse me?" Fear began inching its way into my gut. My heart hammered against my ribcage and I backed up, heading for the window. The lock on it twisted shut, then snapped off. I spun around to find Triarius standing only a foot away from me. Words stuck in my throat, lodged in a scream that refused to come out.

"I promised an interview. I said nothing about having it printed."

# Chapter Two

*"Beth yw e?"*

There was a pause and I heard gravel crunching under shoes. Then a car door slammed, rocking the entire vehicle. I kept still, quiet. If I let on that I was awake, there was no telling what these men would do. I didn't know if Triarius was here, but I remembered enough to know he'd brought me here. Wherever here was.

*"Pam rydyn ni'n aros?"*

I couldn't make out a single word they were saying. I inhaled slowly, hoping to catch any scents that might give away our location, but all I got was the thick, cloying smell of old leather. The car rumbled to life and a moment later, we were moving. Riding was bad enough. Riding while blindfolded, without the ability to look around, sent my motion sickness into overdrive. I fought back the nausea, the low, rhythmic hum of the engine not helping in the least.

Fear clawed at my insides, but if I was going to get out of this alive, I had to stay rational. Panic only led to stupid mistakes, and in the presence of vampires, stupid mistakes meant certain death. I wasn't going to go out without one hell of a fucking fight.

It was night. The cool air blowing into the car from a window up front gave that much away. With my hands bound behind me, I couldn't pull off the blindfold, but I knew the car was big. I was stretched out on my stomach, head facing the front. Words occasionally drifted from the front, but they were still talking in a language I didn't know. I wanted to get the blindfold off, but if I did, they'd know I was awake. For some reason I'd yet to fathom, Triarius hadn't killed me. Why? Why keep me alive when I might find an opportunity to escape?

The air thickened and crispness gave way to the rich smell of earth and stone. I felt the car turn, and then we started up an incline. My equilibrium was off, which made me feel like I was on some sort of carnival ride. I squeezed my eyes shut under the blindfold, more focused on trying to will away the urge to throw up than figuring out where the hell we were to begin with. By the time I got a hold on it, we'd stopped. It took a moment for me to realize we were on somewhat level ground again. The door opened and I willed myself to go limp, hoping it would be too much dead weight for my captors to carry. I hadn't factored them being vampires into my plans when one simply hefted me over a broad shoulder like I was nothing more than a child's rag doll.

We went down steps, then into total blackness. Even if I didn't have the blindfold on, I knew sight would've been pointless. The darkness was a living thing—consuming, almost crushing. It reminded of the shadows around Triarius, the coils that circled and enveloped him. Footsteps and voices echoed off the rock, giving me enough to know that we were in a tunnel of some sort. Sounds were hollow but long, stretching out in front and behind us. My captor, the one carrying me, grunted and shifted me, his shoulder digging into my stomach. My arms ached and my shoulders had long since stopped throbbing and now only burned. I almost dreaded them releasing my hands; I knew the pain of the blood rushing back would be excruciating.

"*Ry'n ni'n gadael yfory.*"

I listened intently, hoping for maybe a familiar word. I didn't know the accents of the men around me. When we stopped, everything grew quiet. Instinct told me we weren't alone, but no one was speaking. A moment later, we continued on. Down more steps, then another tunnel. Finally the space opened up and voices filled the air. More of the same language, though there were other languages mixed in. I thought I heard someone speaking English, but before I could figure out what they'd said, I was carried into another place. Without regard to whether the impact would break my arms, I was dropped onto what I assumed was a bed. Then a door closed.

"*Beth yw'ch enw?*"

I had thought I was alone. I stayed quiet.

"Do you speak English, then? I know you are awake."

"I am."

"What is your name?"

"Lance."

The blindfold was removed and I blinked my eyes open. Soft light filled the room, but it wasn't overwhelming. I looked up and over. A young man stood beside the bed, smiling down at me. He tossed the blindfold to the side.

"I'm going to release your arms. It would be in your best interests to cooperate and not fight me when you are free."

I had no intentions of fighting. I'd need my strength if I wanted to get out of here alive. I nodded. He bent down and unlocked the restraints on my wrists, then set them on the bed. I hissed and ground my teeth together tightly as I moved my arms. Bright, sharp pain bolted through them, from my shoulders to my wrists. I rolled onto my back and blew out a breath, working through the tense aches to get the blood moving freely again.

"Who are you?" I asked the young man as he poured a glass of something clear from a bottle nearby.

He handed me the glass. "It's water." I sat up and took it from him, giving it a cautious sniff. It didn't smell odd. In fact, it smelled clean and clear. "I am Dai. One of Master Triarius' human servants."

Human? I glanced back up at him. "You're human?"

Dai nodded. "A ghoul, but still somewhat human."

"I don't suppose you're going to tell me where I am then."

The smile he gave me wasn't entirely pleasant. "You already know the answer." He pushed away from the wall he'd been leaning against and wandered over to a stone table. "Tell me," he said, finger tracing a grove in the gray stone. "What were you hoping to do with the information he gave you? Did you hope to prove we existed, even though the world knows we do? Did you hope to find clues to our whereabouts so your governments could assist the Romanorum in finding us?"

"No. To all of it. I only wished to dispel the rumors about the Brotherhood—about what goes on down here."

Dai snorted. "Dispel? Oh, I can assure you that the rumors are very much true, Mr. Shaw." I stared at him. "You are wondering how I know your last name." I nodded. "Who do you think set up the interview, Mr. Shaw? Do you honestly think Triarius did it himself?"

"Why did you set it up then?"

"Because you have been a thorn in our side for far too long. Years of speaking with our kind, broadcasting information. Even venerating those who've done the Romanorum justice by serving it without question. By helping them, you are a threat to us."

"What's going to happen to me?"

Dai shrugged and turned for the door. "That is for my master to decide."

"Wait! Where are you going?"

"*We* are going to dinner. Come."

# Chapter Three

The sight I walked in on was something out Dante's Hell. Blood flowed as freely as the wine, and the diners feasted on one another more than the banquet set out before them. A single, long table made of polished stone dominated the room. At its head, Triarius sat, draped in shadows. Candle flames danced across his face, sparking off the silver mask. His pale gaze swept slowly over the others, then rested on me.

"You wished to know more about our kind, Mr. Shaw." Triarius gestured toward the dinner guests. "Join us. Enjoy the veritable feast our cooks have prepared."

I took a deep breath and a cautionary step forward. Only a few looked my way; most simply ignored me. I was grateful for that as I took my place at the only empty place at the table—beside Triarius. He gave me a bit of a smile before lifting a crystal goblet. A moment later, a servant set another matching goblet before me. I stared into the dark, reddish purple liquid.

"It is only wine."

"I take it you no longer enjoy human food?" I asked, looking up at my host.

Triarius sipped at his own drink, and then shook his head. "It holds no interest for me any longer. Though I do admit a fondness for wine."

I picked up my goblet and tasted it. It was sweet and strong, a very good, semi-dry red if I remembered my wines correctly. "It's very good," I said. "A nice bouquet."

"You enjoy wine, then?"

"To a degree. I've never been much of a drinker."

I drank a little more, the flavor growing on me. It really was rather sweet. I could see myself drinking it on occasion. Before I realized it, however, I'd finished the wine. It was the most I'd had to drink in a while, and I almost enjoyed the warm sensation as the alcohol flowed through me. Without my asking, a servant returned and refilled my goblet.

"I must ask, Triarius: what do you intend to do with me?"

"You're taking it quite well that you're here," Triarius answered. Long fingers stroked the crystal chalice in his hands and I found myself mesmerized. Visions of those fingers sliding over my skin drifted through my mind, but Triarius' voice broke through the haze. "I had, in the beginning, the full intention of killing you, Mr. Shaw."

Funny. That didn't bother me as much as I'd expected it to. I watched the way the shadows curled and uncurled around his slender wrists, the tendrils like thin snakes circling his arms. "And now?"

"You intrigue me."

I intrigued him? Here was a man of unbelievable power, undeniable sensuality, telling me that *I* intrigued *him*. I laughed a little, though the sound seemed far away, even to my own ears. "How?"

The shadows entwined around his arms, looping in and out, as if they were alive. Transfixed by their serpentine dance, I wasn't aware I'd finished my wine until the glass was refilled once more.

"You enjoy them."

It wasn't a question, but I nodded. I wanted to touch them, to know what the smoky swirls felt like when they caressed my bare skin. Unable to look away, gaze riveted on the enigmatic creature before me, I sipped at my drink, each swallow easing an ache somewhere deep inside me. I'd never needed anything in my life, so much as I needed to taste *him*.

"Perhaps," Triarius said, though he sounded as if he'd whispered the word in my mind, "we should retire to more private surroundings."

Drunk on wine and the overwhelming need to lap at his skin, I licked my lips. "Yes."

Triarius simply smiled and everyone's attention shifted to the doorway. Brow furrowed, I turned and watched as several young men and women filed into the room. Dressed in flowing robes of crimson and white silk, they glided across the polished floor and stopped in a line, facing the table. When they bowed, they did so in a wave, the effect unsettling, like a serpent. Then they spread out, the men on one side, the women on the other.

One of the women stepped forward, her robe falling away to reveal porcelain skin studded with tiny silver discs in elaborate patterns. The candlelight flickered over her body, the sparkles of the discs dazzling. She danced to a unheard rhythm toward the men, arms beckoning, hips circling, sable hair swaying over her back. When she reached the men, she extended one arm, turned it palm-up, and crooked a finger.

The one to answer was ethereal, as flawless in beauty as the woman. He took her hand, linked their fingers, and drew her up against him. He wasn't hard, which surprised me. I would've been. Individually, they were both beyond words; together, they were intoxicating.

The man turned his partner and cupped the front of her neck, just below her chin. He tipped her head back and licked the side of her throat. Her eyes closed and they began to move, their linked hands moving slowly over the front of her body. Shadows crept up around them, the smoky tendrils snaking up the woman's legs. She parted her thighs, her gasp audible when one of the shadows slipped between them.

I was so enrapt with the display, that I didn't feel anyone behind me until sharp pain burst over my senses. I couldn't move, not when the pain blossomed into something stronger, deeper. Pleasure flooded me with every hungry pull at my throat. I wanted to touch, to feel the body pressed tight against mine. I didn't have to look to know who it was. A sensation in my gut told me it was Triarius.

High on his touch and too much wine, I could only watch and stare when the silver circles on the female dancer's body began pulsing. The pressure on my throat strengthened, my cock filling in my pants in answer, and the woman's cry when she shuddered in her partner's arms left me breathless. I leaned back against Triarius, eyes rolling as I finally gave in. Heat spread in my lap, every throb of my cock met by a low growl from the man behind me.

Spent and dizzy, I slumped back against him, the world sort of fuzzy around the edges. I barely remembered a soft tongue licking my neck, then someone lifting me. A few minutes later, I curled on my side, consciousness slipping away.

# Chapter Four

I don't know how much time had passed, but when I woke, I was alone. I sat up in the bed and looked around the room. It wasn't the same one I'd been in before. The first had been sparse, barren. This room, however, was immaculate: rich, dark woods, polished stone, dark, luxurious fabrics. I was in Triarius' room. I wasn't sure how I knew, but I had a good feeling I was right.

It took me a few minutes to gather the strength to stand. While the effects of the wine had faded, I still had a touch of dizziness. One hand on the end post of the bed, I got to my feet, the room shifting a little before settling. I never got hangovers; that had to have been some strong fucking wine.

There was a tray of fruits on a nearby table. Beside it sat a glass. A note lay on top of the fruit and I went over and picked it up. The handwriting was elegant, unhurried.

*I trust you slept well.*

*You will need to eat something. The fruit will replenish you. There is water as well.*

*I look forward to your company.*

*T*

Something wasn't right. Without the wine muddling my brain, I knew that now. I stared at the platter of fruit. He hadn't taken that much. Had he?

My stomach growling stilled any other thoughts, however, so I grabbed an apple and bit into it. I couldn't begin to stop the groan. It was sweet, needed. I took several more bites, eyes closed while I savored every one. When I finished, I set the core on the table and drank some of the water. I needed more. Hunger was beginning to take precedence. I picked up a pear and started on it, the flavor bursting on my tongue. That one, I devoured quickly. Pangs of hunger clawed at my gut and I chose an orange next. The more of the peel I tore off, the worse the pain got. I couldn't get the fruit into my mouth quickly enough.

One after another, I ate nearly every piece on the tray. The water was long gone. Yet my hunger was stronger than ever, burning its way through my body. I heard voices—outside in the hall, in a room nearby, above me, below me... I doubled over, hand catching the platter before I hit the floor. The metal dish crashed to the stone floor, but I barely heard it. My blood pounded in my ears, heart thundering. Then hands were on me, lifting me to my feet.

His smell. Oh, God. I could smell him—his skin, his breath, his fucking blood. The pain sparked and then my mouth was on his throat, his blood flooding me. I clutched his arms, fingers digging into his skin as I swallowed every precious drop, the hunger finally subsiding.

Soft words that made no sense drifted around me. He stroked my hair and I almost whimpered when the cut healed, cutting me off from the only thing that...

The truth slammed into me and I shoved him backward. Triarius offered nothing but a knowing smile.

"What the fuck have you done to me?" I shouted, backing away from him, toward the door, I hoped. I didn't know.

"You wanted to know more about us—about me," he said, making no move to stop me. "Where will you go, Mr. Shaw?

If you leave, you do so without a supply of my blood. You've tasted me. That is something no amount of words can erase."

"What am I?" Even as I asked, I knew. I didn't want to, but I knew. I wasn't stupid. But oh, God... his blood. I wanted to die, but at the same time, I wanted to drink him forever.

"You know that as well as any other. I cannot have you escaping, and you are much too enticing to kill. What better way to insure you remain by my side—than to give you my blood?"

"The wine." It all made sense now. Fuck. The son of a bitch had spiked the wine.

Triarius nodded. "And now... you can't leave. With my blood in your veins, you are a dead man outside the Brotherhood's protection. Without my blood, you will not survive for long."

"You've killed me anyway."

"Perhaps. Consider it... a trade. My secrets, for your life."

I fell back against the wall, mouth open, my brain not quite processing everything. "I'm your prisoner."

"You are my servant."

I had a life. Not much of one, but I wasn't ready to give it up. "People will know I'm missing."

"No one knew where you were," Triarius countered. "Dai made certain of that. Did you not agree to total secrecy?"

I looked away from him and closed my eyes. I had agreed to it, and for the first time in my life, I chastised myself for being a man of my word. I'd been so desperate for the story, I'd done exactly what they wanted: not told anyone where I was going. No one knew I was here. Eventually, I'd be forgotten as just another reporter lost in the line of duty.

I slid down the wall and rested my head back against it. A quiet resignation followed. A moment later, I sensed him close and when I opened my eyes, he was right there, crouching before me. I hated him. And yet, I wanted him more than anything else in the world. He insured that.

"I am a reasonable man, Mr. Shaw."

I couldn't stop the laugh even if I'd wanted to. "Reasonable? You kidnap me, drag me down to only God knows where, and to keep me here, you essentially sign my death warrant. How is that reasonable?"

"I could have killed you," he said without emotion. "In that room, I could have torn your soul to shreds, rendered your flesh in such ways that no one would ever know what existed before." Shadows slithered out from the corners of the room and circled him. "Do you wish to see what could have happened, Mr. Shaw?"

"No." When I first saw them, those shadows enthralled me. But as they moved, they took on a more ominous presence. I knew, without a doubt, they could kill.

"They are not all for death and destruction." Triarius held out a hand and a thin tendril of smoke stroked his wrist. "Let me show you..."

"Like hell."

The shadow jerked and sliced through Triarius' pale flesh. Blood welled to the surface, weakening my resistance. I fought it, forced myself to remain against the wall, to not move, even when the scent hit me. I squeezed my eyes shut, wanting to block it all out—the shadows, his voice, his scent, his blood.

"You can not run from it," Triarius whispered. "The longer you deny it, the worse the pain of hunger becomes."

I knew that. Oh, God, I knew that. My insides twisted into knots and my mind screamed for relief. With a defeated sound, I grabbed his arm and bit down, sucking hard on the cut. The more I drank, the less I hurt. The more I drank... the more I needed him.

The wound closed and a finger slipped under my chin. I had a split second to stop what I knew was going to happen. I didn't.

Triarius' lips opened over mine and I was powerless to deny him. Soft-spoken in speech, he was someone completely different in this. He devoured me—lips, teeth, and tongue consuming every ounce of defiance within me. One kiss, and I was hard as stone. In one kiss, the most feared and wicked man on earth had me in the palm of his hand.

*"Touch me."*

I reached out, fingertips skimming the arch of his neck. His skin was smooth, flawless, warming under the heat of my touch. Triarius sighed into my mouth, and then stood. He extended his hand to me. I hesitated, knowing what this meant. If I gave in to this, I would have nothing to stand on later. He'd taken everything from me without remorse; he could've taken me by force now. But he didn't.

Meeting his gaze, I took his hand and let him pull me to my feet. Despite how much my mind protested, my body betrayed me. I wanted him—of that, there was no doubt. I went to the bed and he stepped up behind me, hands sliding up under my shirt. His lips moved over my neck, the tip of his tongue tracing a line along my pulse point. He inhaled deeply, a soft hiss of breath warming my skin. Then he pulled my shirt over my head and tossed it aside.

"I've wanted this," he murmured, hands moving down my body. My stomach muscles tightened in response as he neared the waistband of my jeans. Deft fingers popped the button and eased the zipper down. "Since I first saw you in that room. I wanted to taste you."

I bit back the groan that desperately wanted out when his long fingers eased into my pants. My cock throbbed, anticipating. "Why me?"

"Because you are fearless..." Those fingers stroked the tip of my prick and my knees threatened to buckle from just the simplest touch. "You are strong..."

"I don't break," I answered, eyes rolling back as my jeans slid down my legs. Triarius wrapped his hand around my cock and I nearly hit the floor.

"I do not wish to break you."

*No. You only want to drive me insane.*

I fisted my hands at my sides and it took all the will I had to keep from thrusting as he stroked my length slowly.

"I want to test your limits, Mr. Shaw. I want to know how much one man can take before need overwhelms reason."

*Keep that up, and you'll find out really damn quick.*

The movement of his hand quickened. Unable—and unwilling—to hold back any longer, I started meeting his strokes, the defeat heavy with every thrust of my hips.

*Don't stop...*

"Do you taste bittersweet, Mr. Shaw? Or are you strong, the flavor musky and thick?"

"Triarius..."

I felt him smile against my neck. Then he released me. Before I could yell and demand he continue—or finish it myself—he turned me and kissed me hard. My lip split under the assault and his growl filled me, growing stronger as he lapped up the blood. I tried to pull away and he shoved me onto the bed. His robe dropped to the floor and I simply stared.

Black, tribal tattoos covered his chest and snaked down his torso. A single spiral wound its way around his cock, then spread out, up the creases of his hips, around to the back. The patterns on his skin weren't random, but I had no idea what they meant. The lines resembled barbed vines, and they circled each nipple, then merged in the middle of his chest to form an intricate web of sharp angles and coils. Each nipple was pierced, black captive rings begging for my fingers to pull and twist them until he pleaded for me to stop.

Triarius knelt on the bed between my legs and leaned down, licking a path from my neck to my sternum. One hand slipped under the small of my back and lifted me, pressing our bodies together. I groaned and shifted, trying to find some sort of friction for my cock. Unrelenting, Triarius circled my left nipple with his tongue. I gripped his hair, fisting it in my hands, and pressed his face to me. Sharp pain burst over my senses and I shouted, hips jerking against him as he sucked on my nipple.

"Triarius..."

His other hand pushed between us and tightened around my cock, pumping fast. I bucked, breath leaving me as my come poured over his fingers. He released my nipple and licked the bite marks, then slid down my body, cleaning my skin. Hands on the backs of my thighs, he shoved my legs up and with a hungry growl, thrust his tongue inside me.

"Fuck!" My hands hit the bed, knuckles white as I grabbed the blanket. He fucked my ass with his tongue, over and over, the quick stabs driving me crazy. I needed more, needed him to fill me. Triarius pulled back and lifted his head. The smile he gave me should have been warning enough.

Shadows surrounded me, brushing my heated flesh. I watched, utterly breathless, as one long strand drifted over my thigh. Another soon mirrored it, and together, they spread my legs, holding me open, unable to move. My heart hammered in my chest, and the fear returned. Then I felt nothing but fullness.

"Oh, God." I arched, back bowing as another shadow filled me, stretching me open, pushing deeper than I thought possible. I couldn't breathe, couldn't move. Too much. Oh, fuck, it was too much. I wanted to beg him to make it leave, and I wanted more. My body couldn't decide what it wanted, and my brain simply shut down.

Blood dripped onto my lips and I licked it away. Triarius' taste flooded me, heat rising inside. The shadow began to move, fucking me deep and slow. I wanted to fucking kill him, even as I shouted his name, my entire body shuddering as I came.

"Yes."

The word was hissed on my lips, Triarius hovering over me. I lifted my head and took a hard kiss. Triarius groaned, hips rocking and pushing his cock along my ass. The shadows faded, leaving me empty. I refused to beg him, but I didn't have to. I didn't have the chance to ask where he got the lube, because two slick fingers slid deep inside me. I arched and bore down on them, hands digging into his biceps as he finger-fucked me.

He was evil in every sense of the word—my mind knew that. When he filled me finally, however, when his cock replaced his fingers and drove inside my body, I didn't care what he was—only that he was pumping in and out of me with hard, deep strokes. I couldn't catch my breath, and looking up at him, at the mask over the side of his face and those eyes that saw through my soul, only served to hurtle me toward the edge again.

Triarius caught my hands and pinned them to the bed. He nudged my head to the side and a second later, bit down. I bucked wildly, the world graying around the edges as white-hot pain mixed with pleasure enough to nearly stop my heart. I felt his growl more than I heard it, and warmth flooded me, his grip tight on my hands.

When had I slipped so far, that it took a monster to show me what being human meant?

# Chapter Five

"Who are you to him?" I'd been watching Dai for several minutes as he put up clothes in the tall wardrobe near the door.

Without looking up, he folded what looked like a silk shirt and said, "I am his servant, his personal attendant, if you will."

"Are you lovers?"

Dai smiled over at me. "We were—ages ago."

Something eased inside me, though I didn't want to dwell on what, or why. Since last night, I'd fought the urge to seek Triarius out. Instead, I shifted my focus to Dai, hoping he could tell me something about Triarius. "How long have you known him?"

"Hmm..." Dai closed the wardrobe doors and leaned back against them, arms crossed. "Sixty, maybe seventy years? I'm not sure anymore."

"You don't look any older than twenty."

Dai chuckled. "Twenty-one, actually—that's how old I was when we met. As ghouls, we age slower than mortals."

"Did..." I took a deep breath. "Did he change you without consent?"

"No. I was ready to die. A fire destroyed my family home, left me with nothing and no one. He found me when I was at my lowest, and he offered me another life. He needed an assistant, someone who could be his eyes and ears on the outside. I just needed a reason to go on."

"Do you love him?"

"In a way, I suppose. He's my master and I would do anything for him. And he would do the same for me."

I couldn't quite bring myself to believe that. "Somehow, I doubt he would."

Dai tilted his head and grinned. "You don't know the Triarius I do. Despite outward appearances, he is a man of honor."

"Honor."

"Some of his methods might be... unconventional, but when Triarius says he will do something, rest assured that he will do it."

"And ghouling someone without their knowledge?"

"Safety measures," Dai said with a shrug. "You presented a danger to all of us, so we had to stop any chance of your story getting out."

"So I'm a threat."

"Not anymore."

I sighed and fell back onto the bed. "Okay. So he ghouled me to keep me quiet. Why not just kill me?"

The mattress dipped beside me. "Because he wanted you."

"For what? A quick fuck and feed?"

"He's lonely."

I snorted. "You're kidding, right?"

"Do you think humans are the only ones who feel loneliness? Every soul needs a companion."

"Then why not you?"

"Triarius is a great lover, but we found that anything more wasn't for us."

I couldn't deny the lover bit. Triarius ignited something inside me, whether I wanted it or not. I wanted to fucking hate him. He'd stolen my life and my freedom from me. But he'd also given me more pleasure in one night than I'd had in years. How could one man inspire hatred and need in the same breath?

"You're thinking too hard."

"What the hell else am I supposed to do?" I grumbled.

"Do you want a tour?"

I looked over at Dai. "I'm trusted enough to see everything?"

"Well, you certainly can't leave to tell about it."

"Do you always have to remind me of that fact?"

Dai sat up and patted my leg. "Come on. There's much more than just the dining hall and his bedroom."

Sighing in defeat, I got up. "Since I can't leave, can you tell me where the hell we are?"

"Snowdonia," Dai said as he led the way out of the room.

"Snowdonia. As in the mountains?"

He nodded. "The Brotherhood had many homes through the centuries before Triarius finally came down here. The vampires are guaranteed protection from sunlight, it's easily guarded, and honestly, no one knows this cave system even exists."

"Makes sense why he'd come down here, that's for sure." I followed Dai down a narrow stone hallway, but just before we reached the dining hall, he turned left and descended into darkness. "Dai?" My voice echoed back at me. "Dai, where did you go?"

"Come down," he said. He didn't sound nearly as far away as I'd thought. "Be careful—the steps can be slippery sometimes."

"Uh, yeah."

There was no railing, so I did my best with a hand on either side, skimming the walls. The stone steps were damp, but wider than I expected. I went slowly and soon found myself in a vast cavern. Dai stood at a railing and grinned over his shoulder at me. I stepped up to the rail and words simply left me.

"Welcome to the heart of it all, the final headquarters of the Inferi Brotherhood."

It was a city beneath a mountain. Firelight filled the space below us, and niches lined either side of what I discovered was a river. The dark water shimmered as it moved, and people—human and vampire alike, I presumed—were everywhere. Most seemed to have purpose, as they ducked in and out of doorways.

"How...?"

"How did he do it? Triarius had help, of course. One man, god or no, could never do this himself. Humans thrive here with their vampire hosts, and food for them is brought down the river. Where it empties outside the mountain, we have established a stronghold out of castle ruins. It is there that animals and plants are raised for food. Humans are quite industrious."

"You said it was well-guarded. How?"

Dai crooked a finger and beckoned me toward a door to right of the one we'd just come out of. I followed him up more steps. "The Proeliatores are the elite guards of the Brotherhood," he explained. "The first, Triarius trained himself. They, in turn, trained the others, and so forth. Triarius no longer fights with them, though he still has his weapons and armor."

"So he was a soldier?"

"Of a sort, yes. He was a soldier for the Romanorum in its infancy. But it was a falling out with Dio that drove Triarius to create the Brotherhood. He wasn't happy with how the Romanorum ran things."

"Back to the 'god' complex?"

Dai laughed and stopped at a closed wooden door. "You could say that." He pushed the door open. "I must leave you now. He's waiting for you, and I have other matters to attend to."

"But where-?"

"Come in, Mr. Shaw."

I went up the last couple steps and walked into the room. Triarius sat in a high-backed chair at a long, rectangular table. Armed—and armored—guards stood behind him, one at each side. The door closed behind me.

# Chapter Six

"You slept well, I assume?" Triarius waved a hand toward the chair beside his.

"Yes. Thank you." I sat down and a servant appeared out of nowhere with a goblet and a jug. Without thought, I put my hand out to stop her. "No. I'm not thirsty."

Triarius smiled and waved her away. "You still do not trust me."

"Should I?"

He nodded. "A fair question. I do not know how much Dai has told you, but I want you to know that you hold a place of honor here."

I blinked and stared at him. "First, you say I'm a threat and then proceed to change me in such ways that I can never leave this place again. Now, you tell me I have a place of honor? Forgive me if I seem a bit... pissed."

Something crossed Triarius' expression that I couldn't place. "I admit that I have done nothing to warrant your trust, or, for that matter, your loyalty to me. Dai did not agree with my choice to keep you alive. He thought I should be rid of you."

I wasn't sure how to feel about that. Nothing in Dai's actions or words gave me the impression that he didn't like me. "Why did you keep me alive?" Despite having heard it from Dai, I wanted to hear it from Triarius—provided he would even admit to it.

Triarius stood and went over to a window that I assumed looked down onto the area Dai had shown me before. Several moments passed before Triarius spoke again. "I've walked this earth for longer than I care to remember, and while I've always had others around me, I've never let anyone deeper than the surface. I can not afford to be seen as weak."

"Needing companionship isn't a sign of being weak."

"You don't know my world, Mr. Shaw."

Instead of the monster I'd seen before, all I saw standing before me was a man. A wicked, driven man, but a man nonetheless. I stood and went over to him. Taking a chance, I slipped my arms around his waist. I was surprised when he leaned back against me.

"I know I don't know your world," I said. "But I'm willing to learn."

"Why the sudden change of heart?"

I shrugged. "Not so much a change of heart, as admitting that I'm stuck here and I might as well make the best of it. Granted, it doesn't excuse what you've done."

He actually laughed a little at that. "I'm not known for regrets."

"Good." I turned him around and before I could weigh the wisdom of my next move, I kissed him.

Triarius groaned and I smiled against his mouth, realizing I'd surprised him. I reached up and touched his face, tracing the bottom edge of the mask with my fingertips. He closed his eyes and for a moment, I saw beyond the amoral facade. I understood then, everything Dai had said. I didn't have to like it—hell, I didn't have to agree with any of it—but Triarius made more sense than I really wanted to admit. He was right; I didn't know his world.

"You are thinking too hard," Triarius said, startling me out of my thoughts.

"Funny." I laughed. "Dai told me the same thing earlier."

"Then perhaps it is true. You have much on your mind; that is expected."

I sighed and stepped around him, toward the window. Below us, the inhabitants of this city under the earth went on, blissfully unaware of the mortal—or not-so-mortal—in their midst, who was now questioning... everything. As a reporter, I strove to always keep an open mind. I tried to remain accepting, especially of practices and lifestyles different from my own. I was so busy, so driven to uncover the secrets of the Inferi Brotherhood, so intent on the more barbaric practices, that I'd forgotten about the man who'd created it all in the first place—and why he had created it.

Arms snaked around my waist and a kiss was pressed to the side of my neck. Triarius' breath warmed my skin and wherever he touched me; the contact left heat in its wake.

"I'm an idiot."

He chuckled softly. "No. You are human."

"Well, not quite anymore. And..." I stared out the window, not wanting to admit what I was going to say. "I think you are more human than most of us out there."

"Why do you say that?"

"Most humans want wealth and care nothing for others," I said dryly.

"I have no use for wealth, true."

"You created this society because you felt it was the right thing to do."

Triarius laughed. "If it helps you to believe that, then you're welcome to."

I tipped my head back and to the side, peering at him somewhat upside down. "You did, didn't you?"

"I created it because the Romanorum wanted to bow down to the mortals. I am part of the Caelestes family, most of us—primarily the original Brotherhood members—are. We are descended from gods; we *are* gods. Gods do not pay allegiance to mortals."

"Hence using mortals as nothing more than food sources, even to the point of killing them."

He nodded. "I do not apologize for my beliefs or my actions, Mr. Shaw. I do not feel remorse for the lives I have taken, nor for the lives I will continue to take."

"Will you please stop that?"

"Stop what?"

I smirked. "Calling me Mr. Shaw. That's my father's name."

Triarius smiled and cupped the front of my neck, keeping me in place as he lowered his head to brush his lips over mine. "As you wish... Lance."

Sweet fuck. My name had never sounded quite so provocative as it did then. He stole my capacity for speech just as easily as he stole my freedom. Triarius' tongue swept through my mouth, and I was lost. I still hated him for everything, even as I moaned into the kiss, hand going up to slide through his hair. The metal of his mask was cool and smooth, and I wanted to touch it. I wanted to watch the light flicker across it while I rode him.

"Now there is a thought," he murmured.

"Get out of my head."

"I think I'd rather you get out of these," he answered, one hand going down to pop the button on my jeans. He eased the zipper down, then slipped his hand inside. "So hot," he breathed, fingers wrapping around my cock.

I tried to come back with something – anything—but words failed me. I groaned and thrust into his touch, needing more. With his other hand, he pushed my jeans down. "Triarius... what about... oh, fuck..." He pressed his thumb against my slit, the burn sweet.

"Shh, stop thinking."

He bent me forward and I felt him kneel down, his breath hot on my bare ass. Before I could say another word, he spread my cheeks apart and licked my hole. Fire shot up my spine and I moaned, pushing back against his face. His tongue pierced my body and I no longer cared who saw or heard us up here. All I wanted was more.

I clutched the edge of the window, the stone cold beneath my fingers. I closed my eyes and all focus went to the sparks rushing through me with every thrust of his tongue into my ass. Dual sensations kept me off-balance: the touch of skin on one side; smooth, cool metal on the other. My head fell forward, breath panting. His fingers dug into my flesh, holding me open for his torture. If this was my fate, then so be it. I would die to feel this man's touch.

Triarius pulled back and stood, long body leaning over mine. His lips brushed my shoulder blade and he rocked his hips forward. At some point, he'd freed himself and his cock now rubbed along the crease of my ass, teasing me relentlessly. When I groaned and tried to push back, he evaded me, just barely keeping contact.

I hated him even more then—for much different reasons.

"Just feel," he whispered.

Oh, I felt, all right. There was no mistaking the hard cock nestled between my ass cheeks, or the hands on my hips. I licked my lips and bit back a desperate sound when the slick head of his cock pressed against my hole. I held still, every muscle tensed, waiting. With a long, low growl, he rocked, rubbing and pushing, but never quite going in. The man excelled in torture.

"Fuck me, goddamn it!" I snapped, my patience gone.

Triarius stepped back and turned me around, shoving me to my knees. Without a word, he thrust his cock into my mouth. Hands on my head, he pumped in and out, silk steel sliding over my tongue and driving me mad. I looked up and watched his head fall back. I wanted, more than anything, to hear him cry out to me. I needed him to be vulnerable, though I didn't know why. I sucked harder, head bobbing, determined to trip him over the edge. Triarius knew—the son of a bitch knew what I was doing. He pulled out and spun me around roughly, shoving my upper body to the cold stone floor.

"How dare you," he snarled as he thrust his cock deep into my ass.

I didn't have a chance to ask him what he meant. His strokes were hard and brutal, his determination to break me crystal clear. I refused. I rose up onto my hands and slammed back onto his prick, making both of us groan. If he wanted me to fucking break, he'd have to do much better than this.

"Stop fighting me."

"No." I flashed him a glare over one shoulder and a second later, my eyes rolled back as he rammed inside me in response.

I felt like I was playing the devil for my soul, and that only spurred me on. I wanted him to fold, to buckle. I wanted to be the one person who could undo him. Triarius sped up, hips slamming into my ass. His hold on my hips was strong, and I knew I'd have bruises. I could already feel them forming. We both shifted at the same moment then and he nailed my gland. I damn near bit my tongue off when bolts of lightning rocketed up my spine. I didn't have to look back to see the smug grin I knew was there.

There had to be a way to get to him. Searching it, I sat up, the motion driving his cock deep inside me. I let my head fall back against his shoulder and he kissed my neck, fangs just barely scraping the surface. That was it. That was the key.

"Triarius..." I bared my throat to him—in full submission.

The moment he struck, I shot, come splashing onto the stone floor as I shouted his name. Triarius jerked, arms tightening around my waist as he filled me. I felt him shake, and knew—just knew—I'd gotten through.

"Damn you," he whispered gruffly.

"You already did that."

Then he was gone.

I closed my eyes and breathed in deep. His scent was still in the air. I smiled.

# Chapter Seven

"Whatever the hell you did, it must've been good." Dai leaned against the door frame, arms crossed and a wry smirk on his face. "Or really fucking bad."

"We fucked. What else was there to do?"

He snorted. "Yeah. I figured that out when you came back with his scent all over you."

"You're jealous..." I smiled slowly. I wasn't sure why that thought was so appealing, but it was.

Dai's jaw clenched. "I am not," he said finally.

"He said you didn't agree with me being here, that you wanted him to kill me."

He shifted a little and looked away. "Maybe. You were a threat."

I stepped up to him and he glanced at me out of the corner of his eye. "And to you, I still am." Then I went around him and out the door.

Triarius had sent Dai to deliver a message to join him in the throne room. I wondered what sort of reception I'd get, given how he'd left me before. And what of Dai? When I first met him, I didn't see anything about Dai to give me the impression that he was one to watch, but now... I shook my head and followed the directions Dai had given me to the throne room.

It wasn't quite as far as the walk to where Dai had taken me earlier. Without a clock or the sun, I didn't know what day it was anymore, or if it was even day. I assumed it was evening because Triarius was not alone when I walked through the throne room doors.

The room itself was smaller than I'd expected, but the polished, black stone floor made it appear larger. Flames flickered off the surface, lighting the room up further. Stone benches with plush crimson seats lined the walls, and on them sat many vampires—and some humans, I guessed. At the other end of the room was Triarius. He was seated on a throne of dark wood and several armored guards stood near him. In the light of the torches and candles, his mask looked gold. He gestured for me.

"Please, sit." He waved toward a chair at the bottom of the short dais, near his throne. As I sat, he continued. "I trust you slept well?"

"Yes, though I do wonder what day it is."

"That is of little importance. I long ceased to care."

His answers were short, clipped, and I couldn't help but smile to myself. I'd gotten through that damned barrier and found the man behind the devil. I didn't doubt that he was cold-hearted when he needed to be—or even when he wanted to be—but I knew now there was much more to Triarius than met the eye.

"Dai seems to think I've done something terrible," I ventured.

Triarius scowled a bit, though I had a feeling it wasn't necessarily directed at me. "He is spoiled."

"Do you trust him?"

He was so quiet, that I thought he might not answer. Then he said, "I don't know," under his breath.

The admission was a surprise, but I kept it well-hidden. "Why do you doubt your trust?"

"A gut feeling. My instincts are something I learned long ago to trust."

I nodded. That made perfect sense to me. "Can't say that I really blame you. I honestly don't think he likes me much."

"He thinks you've bewitched me."

"Have I?"

Triarius didn't answer and instead waved over a servant. "Would you care for a drink?" he asked me.

"Water?"

"Water, it is."

The servant bowed and hurried out of the room. Despite his attempt to look nonchalant, I could see the lines on Triarius' face, as if he was lost in thought. He'd avoided my question altogether, and that gave me more to wonder on. How could I—a mortal—even begin to control someone as powerful as Triarius? Before I had the chance to dwell on it further, Dai walked into the throne room. I swallowed the groan and schooled my features into something less leery.

Dai strode up to the dais and bowed low. He didn't even look my way. "I've come to collect Mr. Shaw for his evening meal."

Triarius nodded, and then glanced at me. "I will meet you in my chambers when you are done."

I didn't want to leave, especially with Dai, whom I didn't trust, but my stomach was growling. I stood and gave Dai my best smile. "After you."

Without another word, Dai pivoted on his heel and left the throne room. I followed him, grateful for the silence. I figured I pretty much hit the nail on the head earlier when I'd confronted him. I might not have been a threat to the

Brotherhood at large, but to Dai, I sure as fuck was. He seemed to hold a bit of weight with Triarius, but with me here, I had the feeling that changed.

We turned down a hallway and then Dai stopped at a door. He opened it and stepped back, the smile as fake as my own.

"Enjoy your meal."

I didn't answer. I just walked into the room and he closed the door behind me. Only then did I realize something was terribly wrong. I was the only one in the room, and there were no other doorways to be seen. I swallowed hard, and then turned to open the door—only to find it locked.

"Dai?" I knocked on the door. "Dai, the door is locked."

Only silence.

"Dai!" I pounded on the wood with my fists. "Dai! Open the fucking door!"

I heard a sigh on the other side. Then came Dai's voice, though muffled. "I really hate to leave you, Mr. Shaw. There are matters that require my attention. And don't worry, Triarius will not suffer without you. In a few weeks, he'll forget all about you—everyone will."

"Dai!" I screamed.

"Of course, by then, you'll be dead. Have you ever seen a ghoul die, Mr. Shaw? It's a very unpleasant thing to watch. But... you'll find out soon enough. Goodbye, Mr. Shaw."

I banged on the door until my fists bruised. My heart pounded, the sound thundering in my ears. A week. I had a week before my body would need blood. After that...

I scanned the room, searching for any sign of another exit. A single stone table stood in the center. It was the only furniture, and there was no way in hell I could move it enough to break down the door. I thought about kicking the door in hopes it would shatter, but I'd be more likely to wind up with a broken foot. There had to be a way out.

I started feeling the walls, walking the perimeter of the room, hands running up and the smooth stone. If there was another door hidden in the rock, there would be a telltale crack. I spent the next hour and a half going over inch I could reach. Nothing.

Movement just outside the one door startled me and I rushed over to it, slamming my fists against it. "Hey! In here!"

More silence greeted me, then a hiss. I stepped back as blue-gray smoke seeped through the cracks. What the fuck? The vapor rose and I bumped into the table behind me. As it filled the room, it obscured my vision. My eyes began watering and I coughed. The noxious gas swirled around me and made breathing difficult. Then a figure stepped out of the cloud. Or so I thought.

"Triarius?"

I reached out just as I went to my knees. He faded. I shook my head and coughed again. My throat threatened to close in on itself and panic finally set in. I crawled to the door and clawed at it, blood running down my fingers where my nails tore on the stone. My gut tightened and I dropped to my hands and knees, dry heaves starting seconds before the blood.

I opened my mouth, hoping to scream, but nothing came out. The world faded as the smoke filled me.

# Chapter Eight

Something cool touched my forehead and a soft voice intruded on the only escape from hell I had.

"He's fevered but intact." It was a woman's voice. The coolness returned, smoothing across my skin, down my cheeks. She said something else, but I couldn't make it out.

Another touch followed, this one stronger but no less cool. What felt like fingertips ran over my lips, and then lower to trace a line over my throat. I heard a man's voice. It took a moment for recognition to set in.

I opened my mouth, wanting to ask how he'd found me, but a finger pressed to my lips.

"Shh, rest." It was the woman again.

It took a few seconds for my eyes to focus and I stared up into light green ones. She smiled.

"I am Victoria, Triarius' personal physician."

My throat was dry, scratchy. I swallowed convulsively, and then felt someone lift my head a little. A cup was put to my lips and blessedly cool water poured into my mouth. I think I might have moaned. I wanted to protest when the cup was taken away, but I couldn't get the words to form. Darkness slowly took over once more.

* * *

When I next awoke, I knew where I was. On my back, I stared up at the canopy over Triarius' bed. I wasn't even sure how I'd gotten here. The bed dipped beside me and I looked over to find him sitting on the edge. He reached out and brushed a fingertip down the side of my face.

"You know who I am?"

One eyebrow rose and I stared at him. "Of course I know."

Triarius smiled. "Victoria said you might be a little hazy when you woke up. How are you feeling?"

I blinked and looked around. I honestly didn't know how I felt. Everything that had happened seemed like a dream, almost—or a nightmare, rather. I remembered the room, the smoke, Dai's final words.

"It was Dai," I said, looking back at Triarius.

"I know. He's in the dungeon, awaiting trial."

"How did you know?"

Triarius sighed. "When you did not come to me, I knew something was wrong. I went in search of Dai, but I couldn't find him. Before I could send out an order to bring him to me, your pain hit."

"You felt it?"

He nodded. "Your blood is a part of me, Lance."

"What was the smoke?"

"That is a little more difficult to explain... I believe Dai had help, from someone with more abilities than he possesses."

"So it was magic?"

"Yes."

I closed my eyes and breathed in deep. "What will happen to Dai?

"He will be tried. While I do not doubt he is guilty, that guilt must be proven to the other Elders before a sentence can be declared."

Opening my eyes, I stared up at the canopy. "What will his sentence be?"

"Death—by the same means he attempted to exact on you, though much quicker."

"You're going to starve him?"

"Tooth for a tooth," Triarius said. He tapped the mask on his face. "An eye for an eye."

"Can I ask you something?"

"What?"

"You said you wear that due to a sparring match gone wrong. Is that true?"

"Yes... and no." He looked away for a moment. "Not long before I was turned, I found myself on the wrong of the law, so to speak. I survived by stealing whatever I could—food, clothing, objects to sell. I soon caught the attention of a palace guard, and in return for his silence, I offered him my body. The arrangement was better than most. He taught me how to please men, and how to kill. But, as you've found with Dai, jealousy is a deadly thing. Another guard wanted what he could not have. While my lover taught me, I was attacked. I refused to give in, and for my insolence, my attacker took it upon himself to mar my appearance. He hoped it would prevent others from ever wanting me again."

"It didn't work," I said dryly.

"No." Triarius laughed. "It did not."

I leaned up on my arms and watched him. "Take it off?"

His gaze met mine. "It is not a pretty sight."

"I don't care. I've seen worse."

With a nod, Triarius reached up and hooked his fingers on the top edge of the mask. Then he pulled it off slowly. My heart skipped a couple beats when he looked at me.

In sharp contrast to the ethereal beauty of the rest of his face, the right side was grotesque. Deep lines marred the disfigured skin, running from the bridge of his nose, across his eye, and down to the upper part of his cheekbone. The flesh was misshapen and shriveled, and the eye was milky.

"Can you see?"

"With my right eye? No. I am half-blind."

It was miracle he hadn't died.

"How did you survive this?" I asked. I rose up the rest of the way and touched one deep scar.

Triarius drew in a ragged breath. "Luck," he said quietly. "I should have died."

"I know." A part of me didn't want to think on that.

Triarius ran his fingers over the metal mask, remaining silent. I took the mask from him and studied it. It was cool and smooth, inside and out. I turned it over and over, brow furrowing.

"Okay," I said finally. "I give up. How do you keep it on?"

He ran his finger along the outer edge, and a split second later, I shouted and dropped the mask. Blood pooled on my fingers from tiny puncture wounds. I looked at the mask and saw several small barbs, curving inward. Then I glanced up at him. There were no signs of punctures, but then again, they would have healed immediately when he took off the mask.

"I didn't get the mask until after I was turned," he explained. "Until then, I was forced to wear a cloth over the right side of my face. Where I'd been loved before, I found nothing but revulsion after. When I was turned, I vowed to give them all a reason to hate me."

"So you set yourself up as something like a devil."

"Something like that."

I stared down at my fingers and was only partially surprised to see the cuts healing, albeit slowly. "When you carry out Dai's punishment, will you do it in private?"

"It usually depends on the crime. If the crime was directed at the Brotherhood, then the punishment—or execution—is public. But because it was directed solely toward me and you, then it will be private."

"You?" I eyed him warily. "How did it affect you? I'm the one he wanted dead."

"Do you think I would have taken your death lightly?"

That shocked me more than seeing him without the mask. "What?"

Triarius set the mask aside and turned, bearing me back down onto the bed. "Do you doubt me?"

"I don't know..."

His breath warmed my skin, making it difficult to think. "Triarius..."

His lips covered mine and I groaned, opening to him without hesitation. I refused to dwell on the meaning behind his silence, or the knot forming in my stomach. Instead, I drowned myself in his kiss. He growled softly, tongue sweeping through my mouth, devouring every ounce of doubt I had—and doubt I hadn't realized was there.

I cupped his face in my hands, the difference in skin texture fascinating. It drew touch after touch, my fingers stroking as I sucked on his tongue, letting my teeth graze it. Without breaking the kiss, Triarius shifted and knelt between my legs. Still fully clothed, we lay there, content, for the moment, to taste one another's mouths. His breath filled me, and I was dizzy.

"Triarius..." I whispered.

He kissed and licked his way over my jaw, down the side of my throat. I felt his fangs graze my skin and I hissed, thighs spreading as my prick filled. He pressed harder against me, letting me feel how hard he was, how I affected him. I rolled us, surprising him. Straddling his waist, I ground my hips to him, both of us groaning as I rocked on his cock. He gripped my waist and thrust up.

"Need..." My words faltered when shadows opened my pants. I watched, utterly mesmerized, and the shadows dipped inside, taking my breath away when they curled around my shaft. "Fuck," I hissed, bucking into the touch.

"Is that not the idea?" Triarius chuckled.

I wanted to come back with something witty, some smartass comment, but nothing registered except the sensations rippling up and down my length. "Please..."

He lifted me up and helped me to push my pants down. Somehow, I managed to get them off, and in the interim, he'd freed himself. When I straddled him once more, he handed me a jar. I studied it curiously, and then glanced at him.

"Victoria is an accomplished alchemist as well as a physician."

Sounded good to me. I opened the jar and scooped a little bit of the clear gel on two fingers. Then I set the jar to the side and reached back. Triarius' gaze was like a caress, watching me intently as I pushed both fingers deep inside myself. His hold tightened on my hips and his cock swelled beneath me. I thrust my fingers in and out, eyes closing. Then two of his joined them, all four pushing deep, stretching me.

"Fuck!" I threw my head back and rode our fingers, the need for more surging, strong and hungry. "Now. Oh, fuck, now!"

Our fingers were quickly replaced by his cock and Triarius tugged me down, impaling me in one hard, swift thrust. I shouted, hands going to his chest to brace myself as I rode him. He gripped my ass cheeks and spread them open, hips pushing him deep, over and over. I couldn't catch my breath, couldn't speak. All my senses honed in on him—his scent, the relentless strokes driving into my body, the way his very presence enveloped me.

Shadows circled my cock and began stroking, timed to the rhythm of Triarius' thrusts. Caught between the two overwhelming sensations, I was lost. Triarius flipped me and growled, fangs sinking deep into my throat. I bucked and clawed his back, pleasure and sharp pain shoving me over the edge as I came. Triarius followed, his cock throbbing and heat pouring into me, filling my body in a rush.

Breathless and shaky, I collapsed. He licked the wounds and kissed his way back up to my mouth, tongue slipping between my lips. I moaned and tangled my fingers in his hair, the flavor of blood strong. With a flick of his tongue to a fang, he added his own blood, the two mixing until I could no longer tell them apart. Whatever this was, I was powerless to stop it. Hell, a part of me wasn't even sure if I *wanted* to.

# Chapter Nine

We went down to the dungeon, though a part of me sure as hell didn't want to. I'd been in castle dungeons before, but this place was far different. The stench of death was strong. Old death. Pain and despair, rage and madness—it all permeated the rock around us. I couldn't shake the dark feeling that much more went on down here than mere imprisonment.

Triarius and I were joined by several guards, and it occurred to me that, other than Dai, I was the only human down here. One of the guards who led the way, stopped at a door and I peered around him, curious. The door, made of wood and banded in iron, looked heavy, and it emitted an ominous groan as the guard opened it. The smell was even worse, the rush of stale air exhaling out of the hallway before us, nearly knocking me over. I felt Triarius' hand on my shoulder, steadying me, but it was little comfort as we started down the corridor.

I didn't know what I expected, but silence certainly wasn't it. It was so quiet, that for a moment, I wondered if Dai was even still alive. The lead guard unlocked a cell door and stepped inside. When he stood to the side to allow Triarius entry, I realized Dai was definitely alive, but there was a madness in his eyes that I hadn't seen before.

Dai was chained to the wall, his wrists in rusty iron manacles. His hands gripped the chains and I thought I saw dried blood tracing a line down one arm. He was standing, his ankles shackled as well, and his clothes were in tatters, like someone—or something—had shredded them. More blood—some fresh, some dried—showed through the rips in the fabric. His eyes were wide and held an air of wildness and rage that made me take a step back.

"David Bristow, you will appear before the Elders to answer to the crime of attempted assassination of Lance Shaw."

Triarius nodded to two guards and they stepped forward to unlock the manacles from where they were attached to the wall. Dai's ankle shackles were unhooked from the floor and linked together, effectively hobbling him while allowing him to walk with tiny steps. Triarius tapped my shoulder and I followed him out of the cell. Instead of heading back toward the door, however, we went farther down the hall. When we reached another door, he pushed it open. I was surprised to see several other vampires sitting around a crescent-shaped, stone table. All eyes were on us as we entered.

"Go sit," Triarius said, nodding to two empty seats near the center of the table.

Nervousness prickled at my skin as I went around and sat down, yet no one paid me any mind. They were all watching the doorway as the guards dragged Dai into the room. Only then did he start shrieking and screaming. What made it worse, was that his curses and venomous rage were directed at me. Not at Triarius—but at me.

Triarius took the seat next to mine, directly in the center of the table, and leaned forward, hands folded on top of the smooth stone. "Dai, you know why you are here."

"Fuck you!" Dai snapped. Then he shot me a look full of hate. "I'd do it all over again if it meant getting rid of you."

I swallowed, but kept my mouth shut. This whole thing was well out of my league.

One of the other Elders spoke up. "So you do not deny the charges against you?"

"No," Dai snarled. He jerked against the chains and lunged for the table. A hard tug hauled him back into place, the guards gripping his arms so tightly, the skin turned white around their fingers. "You stole my place! You fucking mortal, you stole my position with him!"

I glanced down and saw Triarius' hands tightening where they were linked. Without hesitation, I put my hand down on his thigh, just to let him know I was there. Instinct made me do it; something made me leave it there. His hands eased a bit.

"Why did you do it?" he asked Dai, with much more calm than I expected.

Dai sneered. "I had everything—your ear, your bed, every fucking perk being a master's ghoul. Then *he* came here. In one goddamn night, I lost everything."

"That as it may be," another Elder said, "you attempted to kill your master's chosen."

I blinked. Surely I didn't hear that right. I looked over at Triarius, but his gaze was fixed solely on Dai. Chosen?

"And I'd gladly try again!"

Triarius rose so suddenly, that it nearly threw me off balance. "Enough! Your greed and jealousy has gained you nothing. I trusted you once, but that time is past."

Shadows seeped in through the front corners of the room, sliding across the floor like vaporous, black serpents. Dai's eyes widened and he struggled against the firm hold on him. The closer the shadows got, the more desperate he became. The smoky tendrils slithered up to form a mass in front of him. Then he screamed.

I watched, my blood running cold as ice, as the shadows invaded his body through his mouth. He thrashed wildly, but the guards held on. Dai's eyes turned dark and black lines began forming under his skin. His eyes rolled back in his head. Without warning, Triarius had my face buried against him, obstructing my view. I tried to push away, but then Dai let out a scream that I would never forget.

A split second later, an explosion shook the room. I fought against Triarius when I felt wetness splatter my skin. My heart pounded, nausea overwhelming when the undeniable smell of blood and dead flesh filled me.

Darkness consumed us and when it faded, I shoved away from Triarius, only to find us back in his chambers. Far away from the dungeon.

I stumbled backward until I slammed into the wall, then I slid down to the floor. I couldn't stop shaking, couldn't get that scream out of my head.

"You said you were going to starve him!"

Triarius didn't approach me. "That was the intention. Had he been misguided. But he was in full control of his thoughts and actions."

"He..." I shook my head. "How could you do that? How could you just... tear a man apart?"

"I told you before. My world is far different from-"

I jerked to my feet and stalked over to him, shoving him hard against the wall. "Fuck your world! You're a butcher!"

"Yes!" He pushed me back until I landed on the bed. Then he towered over me. "I *am* a butcher, and a murderer, and a thief. I am also lord of this Brotherhood, and as such, it is my duty to mete out punishment as it fits the crime."

I stared at him, hating him all over again.

"If I soften every time my lover grows squeamish, then I lose the respect of those around me. *That*... is not an option." Before I could respond, he turned abruptly and stormed out of the room, slamming the door behind him.

I stayed there for what seemed like ages. The events of the past several days played out, over and over, in my mind. What had possessed me to dig so deep into the Inferi Brotherhood that I ended up a prisoner of the leader?

I didn't get very far in my thoughts before the door opened again. I was surprised to see the same woman from before – Victoria—enter the room. She smiled and set a tray of vials and fruit on the nearby table.

"Triarius thought you might be hungry."

"Thanks," I grumbled. I fell back onto the bed.

"He is not an easy man to get along with at times," she said, coming up to stand at the foot of the bed. "But he is a good leader—fair. Brutal at times, yes, but fair."

"He's a monster."

"Aren't we all?"

I looked over at her.

"I came to the Brotherhood, not at his bidding, but of my own will. Triarius and I have always butted heads, over some matter or another, but we respect one another. He knows I am good at what I do, and I know, as a leader, he will never steer us wrong."

"How long have you known him?"

She shrugged. "I don't know—thirty years? Long enough to know that the man needs a Valium every once in a while."

I laughed at that. "Yeah. No shit."

"Look, whether he admits it or not, he cares greatly for you."

"I'm sure he does, in his own bizarre, twisted way."

"Lance."

Sighing, I rolled my eyes. "Yeah, yeah. He's a good man, good leader, hot as sin in bed, blah, blah, blah. Tell me something I don't know."

"Okay. How about: he needs you?"

"Uh. Nice try. He needs a lot of things, but I seriously doubt I'm one of them."

The bed post creaked when she leaned against it, arms crossed. "You're his Chosen."

"Okay. What the hell is a Chosen?"

She chewed on the corner of her bottom lip for a moment, then nodded. "A Chosen is a companion, a lover. The only soul a vampire would die for if need be. A soul mate, if you will."

"Die. Somehow, I don't see Triarius ever putting his life before mine."

"You would be surprised. Why don't you go to him?"

I grumbled and rolled onto my stomach, partly to get more comfortable, partly to escape that knowing look directed at me. "He's pissed."

"He'll get over it."

I snorted.

"I'm serious. Go to him, try to accept him—his beauty and his faults. Allow him the benefit of a doubt." When I didn't answer, she sighed. "I have to go. Think about it, and eat. There are two vials of his blood as well. You'll need them."

I stared at the tray of fruit, or rather, the vials of blood. I didn't want to believe that Triarius and I were so wrapped into each other's lives. Getting involved—especially with a vampire—had been something I had effectively avoided for a long time. Too much bullshit, too much headache. But I was also stuck here, caught between death above ground, and the devil below.

*This* was why I never got into relationships.

When Victoria left, I got up and went over to the table. The last time I'd stood here, with fruit in front of me, I hadn't known that I was his ghoul. Now, I knew. Somehow, it made food less appealing. I scowled at the vials, my fingers itching to touch them, to uncap them and swallow every precious drop. Instead, I picked up an apple.

Ignoring the vials, I sat back down on the bed and ate the apple, though I didn't really taste it. I never realized before how much the brain controls taste, but I knew now. Every thought strayed back to Triarius' blood, sealed in thin, glass tubes, beckoning silently. I looked down at the half-eaten apple.

I stood and walked over to the table. The apple in one hand, I picked up one of the vials. There was power in this blood, an end to hunger that no food could ever appease. I set the apple down and opened the vial. Eyes closed, I inhaled deeply, and then turned the vial up.

The sweetest fucking torment was the way this man could take over my senses without even being in the same room. His blood rushed over my tongue and down my throat, blessedly warm, rich. I shuddered and dropped the vial to the tray, then picked up the other. I drank the second one just as quickly, and mourned the loss when it was empty.

I had to find him.

# Chapter Ten

I caught a servant in the hallway. "Where is Triarius?"

"Master is in the baths, I believe. Do you know the way?"

"No."

He smiled. "This way."

We continued down the hall and he stopped just outside a door. "In there, down the steps. Be careful, as they might be slippery."

I nodded. "Thank you." He left and I opened the door.

Heat and steam wafted up the stairwell, making me sweat within seconds of closing the door behind me. A hand on either wall to brace myself, I took the steps slowly, wary of the water. Soft, golden light bathed the bottom of the stairs and when I made the last step down, I found myself in a large room of stone and marble. An oval, yet natural pool was in the center of the room, and in it, Triarius.

I walked over to the edge and sat down, pulling up my pants legs to dangle my feet in the water. It was surprisingly warm, though I figured magic had a good bit to do with the heat more than anything else.

Triarius floated on his back, arms spread out, eyes closed. His mask lay on the edge nearby, as did his clothes. His muscular form captivated me, the scars on his face only adding to his otherworldly beauty. If one could call it that. I certainly saw it as such, I now realized. Despite his questionable morals, the man had captured me in more ways than one.

"Why are you here?"

I started, unaware he'd even known I was there, though I immediately felt foolish for even doubting he would know. "I wanted to see you."

The lower half of his body sank down and I saw that the pool wasn't as deep as I'd first thought. He stood there in the middle, arms crossed over his chest, regarding me with something between curiosity and irritation. I couldn't help but want him, no matter how much the man infuriated me.

"Well?"

"What?" I looked up at his face.

He smirked. "Are you going to sit there all night? Or are you going to get in?"

I scowled at him, pissed that he knew, without a doubt, how he affected me. "Arrogant prick."

Triarius sighed. "Must we revert to such things, Mr. Shaw?"

Jaw tightening, I stood, but instead of undressing, I started for the door. "This was a mistake."

"Lance."

The use of my name, instead of the formality of Mr. Shaw, stopped me. I closed my eyes and took a deep breath. He was a proud, monstrous, son of a bitch... but that didn't stop me from falling.

Goddamn it.

Arms slid around my waist and a wet body pressed up against my bare back. I didn't lean, but I didn't pull away either. "What am I to you?"

"My Chosen." The words were whispered in my right ear and Triarius kissed his way down my neck. "My lover."

I shivered and barely managed to bite back the moan when his lips found a particularly sensitive spot on my neck. "Triarius..."

"Join me." His hands descended, deft fingers working open my pants. They slid down my legs and pooled at my feet. "I would never harm you, Lance."

His hands almost burned where they touched the front of my upper thighs, just close enough to my crotch to make me bite my tongue to keep from begging. I knew he wouldn't hurt me. I didn't know why I knew that; I just did. Oh, God, I wanted him...

"Come," he murmured. "Join me in the water, let me prove myself to you."

"You don't need..." My eyes rolled back when he cupped my balls in one hand, rolling them gently. I tried to finish, but couldn't remember what the hell I was going to say. I spread my thighs and pushed back a little, groaning when I felt his cock, hard and hot, pressing against my ass.

I stepped out of my pants and let him walk me back toward the pool. Then he turned me around to face him. He studied me just as intently as I did him.

"You are stubborn and have an uncanny knack for irritating me."

I laughed and shook my head. "Like you're one to talk."

He smiled at that. "I won't deny it. I know I am not an easy person to deal with at times."

"I guess we're evenly matched in that regard, then."

Triarius cupped the back of my neck, pulling me a little closer until our lips were a breath apart. "That we are."

Impatient, I closed the distance, kissing him hard. So what if he drove me insane? So what if he killed? We came from very different worlds, and yet that didn't stop me from falling in love with the man. A step back and we both hit the water. I caught my breath at the last second before going under, and then swam back up to find him waiting for me. He pushed me against the edge and kissed me again, hands on either side of my face, keeping me from moving.

Like I really wanted to be anywhere else but here.

I sucked on his tongue and was rewarded with a low groan. His cock throbbed alongside mine, and I wrapped one leg up around his hip, tugging him closer. Both of us gasped into the kiss as our cocks pressed tightly together, the friction beyond words. Triarius pulled back for a moment, rocked his hips into me, and then crushed our mouths together again. I dug my fingers into his shoulders, and then relied on the water and his strength to hold me up as I wrapped both legs around him.

"I have nothing to slick the way," he mumbled.

"Don't care." I just wanted that cock inside me—now. "Please."

Triarius reached down and rubbed the head of his prick over my hole. Holding my ass cheeks apart with his hands, he thrust up, driving his cock deep inside me.

"Fuck!"

"That's the idea," he grunted, hips pumping that thick cock in and out of my ass.

All I could do was hold on, watch his eyes. Everything was there—every fucking bit. He didn't need to say it; I just knew. I threw my head back, breath leaving me as he filled me over and over. I wanted to beg for more, and I wanted to beg to come. His strokes were deep and hard, but at a torturous, slow rhythm. I couldn't get enough friction to get myself over the edge. Then he sank his fangs into my throat.

Shouting and bucking, I came hard enough to see stars, hard enough for tears to burn my eyes as I squeezed them shut. Triarius slammed into me, faster now, then stiffened. The growl vibrated my entire body, from my throat to my ass, as he came deep inside me.

Sweet fuck, I was so lost.

It took a few minutes before either of us could even think clearly enough to move. He pulled out and I let my legs fall back down. Triarius rested his forehead to mine, his eyes closed. His hands remained on my waist, my arms draped over his shoulders. I breathed in deep, drawing him into me. It wasn't the first time I'd fallen so quickly, but I'd sworn I would never do it again. I didn't even know when I'd finally fallen in love with him, and a part of me hated myself for doing it so quickly. Yet another part found a sort of peace, strangely enough. I laughed a little at the thought.

"What?" His eyes were still closed, but he looked more relaxed than he had when I first came in.

"Just thinking."

"About...?"

When I didn't answer right away, he opened his eyes and stared into mine. At such close proximity, it was a bit unnerving. His slight smile dissolved that, however.

"Dai accused me of bewitching you."

"In a sense, yes."

"Are you sure it's not you who has bewitched me?"

I felt one of his eyebrows lift. "Why would you say that?"

I swallowed and looked away. Fingers cupped my chin and turned me back to face him. The compassion and knowledge in those eyes unsettled me more than any horrible thing he could ever do. Then he smiled and kissed me.

I could've handled a hard, hungry kiss much better than the one I got. This one was soft, almost reverent. It unraveled me. Kisses like that made me say stupid things, like...

"I love you."

Only then did the kiss take my breath away, Triarius thrusting his tongue into my mouth and taking possession of every ounce of me. I cursed myself even as I gave in to him completely. He lifted me and put me on the edge of the pool, leaning me back. Standing between my legs, he kissed his way up one thigh, then the other, taking great care to avoid everything higher. I groaned and spread my legs.

Triarius moved up, finally, and licked a path from the base of my cock to the tip. I slid my fingers through his hair, wanting more. He lifted my cock and circled the head with his tongue. The motion drove me insane and I growled, thrusting deep into his mouth. He moaned around my prick, sucking hard.

"Fuck!" I pumped my cock in and out, holding his head still as I fucked his mouth. "Don't stop. Oh, fuck..."

Hips jerking, I shot down his throat. He licked me off, kissed the tip of my cock, and sank back down into the water. I just lay there, boneless. Dear God, the man was talented.

# Chapter Eleven

"There are things I do not speak of freely. Things that others could never understand."

After our time in the pool, we went back up to the room overlooking the underground city. Triarius leaned out the window, hands braced on the sill as he stared down at the flurry of activity below. I sat in the chair behind him, listening.

"You've had no one to confide in, not even all this time you've been alive?"

He shook his head. "I do not trust easily."

"Why trust me?"

"A kindred spirit, perhaps? Something I can't pinpoint, but know in my soul."

I had the feeling it was the closest I would get to any sort of admission on his part. I couldn't imagine surviving that long, without a soul in existence to talk to, even if only idle chatter. Triarius struck me as the type to avoid idle chatter, though. Still, it had to suck.

"So what happens now?" I asked him. "If Dai didn't accept me, then what makes you think anyone else will?"

"Dai was corrupted. Twisted."

I bit my tongue. Those words seemed a bit... odd, coming from a man like Triarius. "What does that have to do with the others?"

Triarius turned to face me. "The word of the Elders is law. My word is law. With the Elders behind us, your presence will never be questioned again."

It took a moment for what he said to sink in. When it did, my mouth dropped open and I stared at him. "Wait. You... you're talking about me... at your side. Not just a lover."

"Co-ruler, if you will."

I blinked. "Co-ruler. You're kidding." He shook his head. "But I know nothing about ruling—anything. I don't know anything about your world, the Brotherhood. Hell, I know only a tiny bit about the Romanorum."

"What better time to start learning?"

I thought about it for a few minutes. I was certainly here for the long haul, so what other choice did I have but to embrace, more or less, my new-found position. I hadn't really expected him to make me co-ruler, but I couldn't deny the fact that a part of me was thrilled. It gave me a sense of power, even though it was nowhere near Triarius', or the Elders'. But still, it was power.

"All right," I said, nodding. "Teach me."

Triarius smiled and walked over, extending his hand. "Come. I want to show you the world I've built."

I took his hand and stood. "After you."

We went out and down a set of steps I hadn't realized was there, to the left of the door. When we reached the bottom, we were on one side of the dark river I'd seen from the landing above. Several people—humans and vampires—stopped and bowed when they saw us. Triarius nodded at them in turn, leading me down the path. On our left sat a row of what looked like caves. Fires burned in many of them from central circles. Pottery stood stacked along walls, wooden furniture filling the spaces. Thin, tattered cloths covered windows, though the doors remained open. Across the water, I thought I saw a blacksmith's shop, and even a grocer. A single wooden boat floated in the river, tethered to a post.

It amazed me how efficient, how structured everything seemed to be. Everyone had a job, and they all went about it with purpose. It really was a city beneath the mountains. Primitive, but fully functional and self-sufficient.

Triarius pointed to the cave the river flowed through. "Just on the outside, there is a stronghold. Farmers work the land, raise livestock, and do most of the processing there. They send the products down the river on small barges."

"Don't you worry about the farmers and those patrolling the stronghold? What if they decide to turn you into the Romanorum?"

"The humans who stand guard and those who farm, all belong to the Brotherhood. Most of them are ghouls to other vampires here, some even to the Elders."

"Okay, that makes sense. Put those you trust—those with something to lose—in charge of that area. So if they go to the Romanorum, they are doomed to die as well, so they've gained nothing."

"Precisely."

"So, what about the Elders?

"Well..." Triarius stepped aside when two women came down the path, carrying a large basket of fruits. He smiled and nodded at them before they stepped into one of the spaces. "The Elders already know you are my Chosen. As it is within the Romanorum, we in the Brotherhood follow the practice of co-rulership when choosing a companion."

"Master Triairus!"

We both looked up at the young woman calling from the landing above.

"The others are ready, Master," she said.

Triarius nodded and waved toward the steps we'd come down. "Shall we?"

I led the way back up the steps and down to the landing. The young woman was gone. "Where'd she go?"

"Oh, probably back with her mother."

"Mother?" I followed Triarius to the throne room.

"Victoria. Marie is her daughter—in the vampiric sense. No familial relationship beyond Victoria having turn Marie about twenty years ago. Marie is also her assistant."

Triarius opened the throne room door and stepped aside for me to enter. The Elders sat on benches around the room and Triarius went up to the dais. I was surprised to see a smaller throne-type chair beside his. He smiled and motioned to it. I went to him, and then sat down. It felt odd being up there, the subject of all those gazes around me. Yet none of them seemed malicious. If anything, I felt like they all supported us—or at least, they supported Triarius' decision. Whether they supported me specifically, I figured time would tell.

"You all know why I have brought you here," Triarius said from where he stood in front of his throne. "You all were witness to the trouble Dai brought down when he objected to my choice. Let it be said: if any man here objects to my choice of companion, then leave now."

I looked around, but no one moved.

"Then let me formally introduce my Chosen, Mr. Lance Shaw." He looked back and held out a hand.

Taking it, I stood and bowed a little. Much to my surprise, everyone clapped. It helped to ease the worry inside me. We both sat back down and the throne room doors opened. Servants appeared at our sides, offering Triarius a cup, of blood, I assumed. For once, I took the wine offered to me without question. I stared into the dark red depths, then over at Triarius.

"You only need to ask," he said. Then he bit down onto his own wrist and held it over my cup as the blood dripped into the wine. The cuts healed and he took a sip of his own drink.

I closed my eyes and drank, almost moaning when I tasted him just beneath the flavor of the wine. Sharp, sweet, powerful. When I opened my eyes once again, the room filled with dancers. I smiled when I recognized the woman and man from my very first night here.

The woman came up and made a low bow before us, then turned to her partner. As if dancing to silent music only they could hear, they began moving. Their rhythm was much like it had been before: slow, sultry, erotic as hell. She circled her partner while he stood in the center, cock hard, her fingers dancing along the length. She licked his shoulder, drifted behind him, and stopped.

Heartbeats passed.

Then she bit down, fangs piercing his throat. From out of nowhere, dancers surrounded them, men and women, kissing, touching, licking... The man in the middle tipped his head back, eyes closed as another man knelt down and swallowed his cock. Women flanked them, hands sliding over the man's chest, their fingers linking when they met in the middle. The man cried out, hips jerking.

I watched in amazement as wings unfurled from behind him. Horns emerged from his hair, teeth turned to fangs. The female dancer circled back in front of him, to face us. The discs on her body shimmered. Arms spread, she tipped her head back and dropped to her knees, body shuddering as she transformed into from female to male. I was mesmerized.

"Now you see," Triarius whispered in my ear. "We are much different than your world."

"Yes..."

"You can have this," he said, waving his hand toward the dancers. "You can learn to do these things."

"How?"

"By becoming one of us."

I looked over at him. "What?"

"Let me turn you."

"I thought you wanted me to remain human, someone who could go to the outside if need be."

"That was my intention, before..." He smiled slowly. "Will you do it?"

I glanced back at the dancers, with their bizarre rituals, their shifting forms. Was I willing to give up my humanity, to become like them, like Triarius? Being his ghoul had its perks, namely that I was off-limits should anyone think to let jealousy take over their reason. I wanted to learn. Whether or not I ever reported another news story again, my curiosity was insatiable. Sometimes to my detriment. Then again, sometimes not.

"Okay.

A tray was brought to me, and on it sat a small vial. I knew—somehow knew—what it was. Vampires couldn't turn without a formula to join the blood. I also knew that if I killed a mortal after this, my soul would forever wear the mark. A few days—a week?—or so ago, I would've fought with everything I had. Now, I only wanted to be a part of this world. If Triarius' plan had been to draw me into the Brotherhood, then he had succeeded.

I took the vial and the servant stepped away. When I looked up from studying the viscous liquid, Triarius was standing before me.

"Come. Join me."

When I stood, he pulled me close and shadows swirled, engulfing us. I clung tightly to him, too startled to ask anything. When the shadows left, we were in his room. I eased my hold and looked around.

"Wow. Neat trick."

"Something you will learn to do in time." He cupped my chin and tilted my face up for a kiss. "On the bed."

I stepped back, hit the edge, and fell backward. He came down with me and took the vial from my hand. Then his lips were back on mine, the kiss deep but unhurried. One hand ran down my side and gripped my hip, pressing us together.

"If you change your mind, do it now."

"No. I'm ready."

He picked up the vial and uncapped it. Then he bit his wrist and held it over my mouth. I caught his arm and drank, prick hard as stone but my mind solely on the flavor bursting over my tongue. We both groaned, and he pushed against me, over and over, hips rocking until I cried out, the sound muffled by his arm, as I came. Triarius gasped, jerked hard against me, and I watched his eyes roll back a little, felt his cock throbbing beneath his pants.

Then he pulled his arm away and tipped the vial over my mouth. I swallowed, ignoring the weird, almost caustic taste. When it was gone, he slit his wrist against and fed me more blood.

The pain hit then.

It slammed into me, twisting my insides into tight knots. I tore away from his arm and screamed, my throat closing. Clawing at my neck, my clothes, I thrashed on the bed, body seizing. I felt Triarius pin my arms down, his strength overwhelming. Still I fought. I knew I was dying, I knew it was necessary. But, oh, God...

"Stop. Let it happen."

"Triarius!"

I bucked, the world fading fast. I tried to get him off of me, but the deed was done. I felt my heart, my entire body, dying—and there was nothing I could do to stop it now. With a final scream, I gave in.

# Chapter Twelve

*A few days, or nights, later...*

The first sight to greet me when I woke was Triarius. He hovered over me and smiled.

"Welcome back."

"I'm hungry." It was the only thing on my mind—a gnawing, piercing hunger that twisted my gut.

Triarius helped me to sit, then made a slit in his own throat. He drew me to it and I groaned when the scent of his blood hit me. Without thought, I latched on, the sensation of my fangs sinking into his flesh diminished in the rush of blood over my tongue. I drank deep, sucking, fingers digging into his shoulders. He moaned and cupped the back of my head, pressing me tighter to him.

All I wanted was more. Fuck, he tasted good.

Somehow, he freed himself from me, and I growled in response, fangs bared, his blood on my lips.

"Shh, there will be more."

The door opened and Victoria came in, carrying a tray with several bottles. She set the tray on the bed beside me, smiled, and left again. Triarius opened one of the bottles and handed it to me.

"Drink. It's mine. Taking any more from me will push me to feed, as well."

I grabbed the bottle and tipped it up, nearly choking on the blood but not caring in the least. By the third bottle, the hunger had finally dissipated. I collapsed back onto the bed as Triarius set the tray on the floor. Then he stretched out beside me. I didn't question him when he wrapped me in his arms. This was where I needed to be—now, and forever.

"Forever is a long time," he whispered.

"Yeah, it is."

"Are you certain you can handle me for that long?"

I laughed and looked up at him. Only then did I realize he wasn't wearing his mask. Come to think of it...

"You... you haven't worn it since the pool..."

"No."

"Why did you wear it, honestly?"

"People modify their bodies in many ways, for many reasons. Some do it for art, some for the pain. And some, like myself, do it to hide from themselves. Self-loathing is a strong bedfellow to self-abuse."

"And the mask, its barbs... They were a way for you to remember what happened."

"To remind me that I am no longer beautiful."

I smiled. "Don't you think it's time to acknowledge the fact that you are, despite appearances?"

His brow furrowed. "I do believe you are blind," he said dryly.

"Nope." I rolled us until I was on top, straddling him, looking down at a face I'd grown to love in a very short time. "While everything else might have changed in me, my eyesight is perfectly fine." I leaned down and kissed a scarred line just below his right eye. Triarius' hands tightened on my waist.

"I am not perfect. I never will be."

"I don't want perfect..." I kissed along the line, then down to his lips. "I want you."

"You have me."

"I want *everything*, Triarius."

His hands left my waist and came up to cup my face, lifting my head until I was looking into his eyes. "You have it, Lance."

I did. I saw it his eyes. I smiled and kissed him again, knowing full well what he left unsaid. He moaned softly, hands sliding back down to my hips, pulling me down onto him. I rocked, licking his lips, cock filling. His was hard, pressing against my ass. Triarius slipped his hands down into the loose pants I wore and pushed them over my hips and ass. Then he spread my cheeks, fingertips tapping against my hole.

"Please," I murmured, pushing back. "In me."

One hand left and I attacked his neck as he shifted to reach the oil. Just as I grazed his throat with my fangs, two slick fingers slid deep into my ass. I groaned and thrust back, driving them deeper. He stroked them over my gland and sparks shot behind my closed eyelids. Then the fingers were gone and I lifted up so Triarius could shove my pants down and off. I settled back onto him and sat up, sinking down onto his cock.

"Oh, God..." Hands on his chest, I rode him, slow and easy.

Triarius watched me, his hold on my hips strong, every rock of his body going deeper. "Lance..."

I sped up, leaning down as he drew his legs up. He thrust harder, faster, forcing my breath out of me. "Fuck. Triarius. Don't stop."

"Never." Fingers digging into my skin, Triarius pumped in and out of my body with enough force to make the world spin. "Lance."

I opened my eyes, right on the edge. "Please..."

One hand came up and fisted in my hair, tugging me down for a deep, hungry kiss, the words "I love you" growled against my lips.

I shouted, eyes going wide as I came. He followed right behind me, pinning me down onto him as his cock throbbed, heat pulsing deep into my ass.

I collapsed, panting. "Holy..."

Triarius nodded and I felt him kiss my head. "Indeed."

"Did... did you mean it?" I lifted my head to look down at him.

Triarius smiled. "I did. Never thought I'd say it, but it's true. Do you still think me a monster, a devil?"

"No, but you can still be infuriating."

He chuckled and flipped us, putting me on my back. "I do believe, Mr. Shaw, that you've warmed up to me."

"Enough to see the man beneath the mask, and not the evil I thought he represented."

"Do you still regret your decision to interview me?"

"No. You've opened up my eyes to a world I never really knew, one that I wouldn't have understood if you hadn't brought me down here." I stroked a fingertip down the right side of his face, but this time, he didn't flinch. "And I thank you for that."

"Will you wear my mark?"

"Mark?"

He seemed to think for a few seconds before answering. "Something akin to a tattoo—a sigil, a brand. It shows that you are mine, and I am yours. The process is painful, but as a vampire, your body can withstand more pain now that it could before."

"Then yes, I will," I said without hesitation.

Triarius placed his palm on my chest, just over my heart. "Mine." The second the word was out, fire burned into my skin, searing and painful. I shouted, back arching as the heat rushed through me. Then it faded. When Triarius lifted his hand, a golden sigil, the same one tattooed on his breastbone, was now etched into my skin.

"Yours."

*Legends of the Romanorum, Book 4*
Sight Unseen

# Chapter Thirteen

The otherworldly, electronica beats of Beborn Beton filled Yesterday's Memories—the antique shop Jamie Smith ran—from the CD player sitting on the countertop. It had been a slow day, and now it was just after sunset, close to quitting time. This early in the week, Jamie was taking the opportunity to get some of his reading in. The noise from traffic outside was muted in the store, leaving Jamie able to concentrate on his book . His laptop was open beside him, allowing him to occasionally double check the availability of ingredients at his favorite downtown herbal store.

The brass bell over the door jingled and for a brief moment, the hum of traffic and blare of car horns poured inside before the door closed again. A middle-aged man walked up to the counter, eyes hidden behind dark sunglasses. Dressed in khakis and a dark green, button-down shirt, he looked like everybody else who occasionally walked through the door of Yesterday's Memories—average build, not exceptionally tall but not short, red hair. Overall, nothing stood out about him, except for maybe sunglasses indoors .

"Excuse me, but I'm looking for Jamie Smith."

Timothy, Jamie's spectral companion, drifted from the back room. "Oh, nice vamp. If I had a body, I'd do—"

Jamie closed his eyes in irritation and cleared his throat noisily before Timothy could finish. Whether or not the vampire could see Timothy depended on whether the creature had had the power when he was alive. At the moment, Jamie prayed he didn't. Ignoring Timothy, Jamie smiled politely and said, "I'm Jamie Smith. How can I help you?"

"I'm looking for this," the man said, sliding a faded picture across the counter. He turned his head toward the far corner, but said nothing before looking back at Jamie. "Have you seen it?"

Jamie started nervously when he saw the picture. He stared at it, hesitating in his answer. Timothy hovered behind his shoulder to get a closer look. "It's that the piece you don't like to touch," the spirit said.

Jamie glanced up at the man. "Yeah, I've got it. You interested in it?"

"Yes. It belongs to someone and I've come to retrieve it. Has anyone touched it?"

"Retrieve it?" Jamie scowled, immediately wondering if somebody was going to try to sue him over the thing. "I keep it in a case, so I'm the only one who's touched it."

The man cursed under his breath. "Give me your hands."

"Excuse me?" Jamie moved away to the other end of the counter than opened the back of the display case and pulled out the jewelry box. "If you want to buy the necklace, it's going to cost you two grand. It's genuine pearl."

The man grabbed Jamie's wrist before Jamie could open the box. "Do not touch it."

"I think you need to back off before I call the cops." The stranger was really starting to piss him off. "And let go of my arm, now."

"That might not be—" Agitated, Timothy hovered as close as he could, but he couldn't do much.

"Timothy, just shut the fuck up, all right?" Jamie snapped.

A spark flickered up through Jamie's arm and the man released him. "Who else has been here?"

"Been here?" Jamie edged away, closer to the phone. "Look, why don't you just leave? I'm about to close shop, and I'm not in any mood to do business with you."

"You don't want to walk away from me. I'm willing to pay you—others won't be."

"Maybe you shouldn't sell that thing." Timothy whispered in Jamie's ear. "Something is going on."

Jamie opened the box and studied the necklace made of black pearls interspersed by bloodstones. Why would a vampire be interested in this? The other guy who had been in the night before hadn't had the cash at the time to meet the price Jamie wanted, but he'd said he'd return. Lost in thought, Timothy absent-mindedly touched one of the pearls. A sudden rush of dark power sent him staggering backward, blindly trying to stop himself from falling. Something exploded in his head and he crashed to the floor, toppling over several of the antique music boxes on a shelf behind him.

Within seconds, hands were on him, helping Jamie to sit up. "I told you not to touch it," the man hissed.

Jamie barely heard him. He blinked, but he saw nothing but darkness. When the shadows faded, he wasn't in his own store anymore. Shock rippled though him when he saw himself surrounded by people, their dress definitely from the turn of the millennium. Then came the heat. Flames flared up, dangerously close to his bare feet. Jamie screamed and fought against the ropes binding his wrists behind the wooden post. The ropes burned into his skin, the cloying smell of wood, smoke, and burning flesh strong.

An unseen force slammed into his chest, followed by a flash of blinding light, and he found himself on a boat, the sea churning, the gales threatening to capsize the small vessel. More lightning flashed and Jamie gasped, going to his knees on unforgiving stone. In the filth-ridden alley, he heard people and animals, bells chiming in the distance. Then blackness filled his vision once more. He heard someone speaking to him, the sound of the voice far away.

"Jamie! Jamie!" The screech of Timothy's voice calling him broke through, and Jamie opened his eyes to see the vampire kneeling beside him and Timothy right behind him.

"Haridan. Your name is Haridan."

The vampire nodded and cupped Jamie's head, thumbs on his temples. "Don't fight me."

Jamie wasn't in any position to fight. He felt the pull at his consciousness trying to drag him back into the life he'd just experienced, and he fought it, forcing his mind to blank and allow the vampire some access. Sharp, intense power flooded Jamie, shielding him from the necklace's energy. The two forces tugged at him until the vampire won out, pulling Jamie back into the present. The transition jolted him and he gasped, sucking in a quick breath.

"Don't touch it."

To Jamie, it nearly felt like being torn in two mentally. He'd been connected to another's life, and had become Haridan in those moments. Trying to stop the dizzying sensation in his own head, he blinked. The memories were still there—Haridan's memories. "Destroy that fucking thing."

Timothy crouched on the other side of Jamie. "Are you all right?"

"I'm fine, Timothy. Don't worry."

"I can't," Haridan said. "It's not mine to destroy. I was only sent to-" Shadows engulfed them suddenly, Haridan trapping a pocket of air for Jamie, just as the front door shattered. Glass flew across the room and feet crunched on broken glass. Haridan clamped his hand down on Jamie's mouth.

"Find that damn necklace!" one of the intruders shouted. Then they began tearing the place apart, smashing antiques and glass.

"Not a sound," Haridan hissed softly in Jamie's ear.

Neither Jamie or Timothy said a word. Jamie stiffened. He now knew how dangerous the necklace could be. He couldn't see the destruction, but he could hear it. His entire livelihood, every single piece, crushed to dust.

"It's not here!" Shattering glass followed the growl, then the crash of the cash register hitting the floor.

"He must've taken it home," another of the men said.

After a few seconds of silence, the first thief said, "Then we'll pay Mr. Smith a little visit."

When the place fell into an uneasy quiet once more, the shadows faded. Haridan released Jamie. "You're in danger. Even if I took the necklace, they'd hunt you down. You've touched it; that's enough."

Jamie carefully eased himself into a sitting position, staring at Timothy, whose form shifted in and out of focus, the look on the spirit's face worried. He didn't think Haridan hearing him speak to the ghost at this point would matter. "Timothy, just calm down, please. You're not helping any."

"But he's right," Timothy whined. "You've got to get out of here, Jamie. I ain't hung around this long to see you turn into a ghost."

"I'm not going to be a ghost." Jamie grabbed the metal edge of the counter while trying to avoid the shards of glass from the display case, and got to his feet.

Haridan stood and helped him to steady. "You can't go home. And reassure your spirit friend that I won't let you become a ghost."

"No, you can't go home," Timothy blurted. "He's the only one who can protect you."

Jamie glared at Timothy before he looked back at Haridan. "He thinks you're the only one who can protect me."

"From them? I can guarantee it, unless you make it a habit of picking up vampires on a regular basis. Even then, no one knows the necklace has been stolen, Jamie. The others will hunt you and invade you to pick out every shred of information—about the necklace, about me..."

Jamie could almost hear Timothy's head rattling in agreement. He rubbed at his forehead, trying to think straight, but it didn't help. "Let's just get the hell out of here. Then I'll figure out what to do."

"Is there anything you need before we leave? We can't come back, and we can't go to your home."

Jamie stared blankly at the ruins of his store for a moment. "I need my receipts. In the safe." He went into the back room, opened the safe, and got the receipts. When he returned to the front, he quickly picked up several pieces he absolutely refused to leave behind. "We can go now."

Haridan grabbed the box with the necklace. "Come here and hang on."

Jamie eyed him askance and cautiously took the vampire's hand. He severely regretted it when the blinding darkness engulfed them along with sickening sense of speed. If he was lucky, he wouldn't puke on his bizarre rescuer .

# Chapter Fourteen

When the shadows faded, they were in a room—a hotel room, from the looks of it. Haridan set the box on the table and went to double-check the locks on the door and the windows. "We're safe here. For now, anyway."

Jamie somehow doubted Haridan's word. He grabbed for the nearest wall for support, feeling his stomach rebel against what he'd just went through. "Want to warn me next time?" When he straightened, he noticed Timothy had somehow tagged along for the ride. "How'd you—?"

"Hey, I'm a ghost. I can do what I want."

"Yeah, you can do anything but be useful," Jamie shot back, earning himself a laugh from the wraith for his trouble.

"Sorry." Haridan stripped off his long coat and tossed it over the back of one chair. Then he removed his sunglasses and set them on the table as well. Haridan's eyes were green, but a shade Jamie had never seen in human eyes.

Realizing from what'd he experienced from Haridan's life that the vampire was blind, Jamie studied him silently for a moment. "That was your life. I can't even begin to understand what I saw."

Haridan sighed. "Yes. You saw glimpses of my life, traumatic experiences mostly. It's one of the necklace's powers. When touched in the presence of a vampire, it shows his or her life—and his or her weakness. You saw mine."

"It's still in my head. Things about you, but now I'm not seeing it like it's really there." Jamie was doing his best to understand and try to remain relatively calm, but this was way outside of his experience level. He'd never really dealt with vampires before. Ghosts were the closest he'd ever gotten to the dead.

Sitting on one of the two beds, Haridan leaned back, propped up on both elbows. Blind or not, those unreal green eyes were fixed on Jamie, as if the vampire could see him in other ways. "I lost my sight due to fever when I was six. When I was seventeen, I was accused of poisoning the livestock and the crops of my village. The local priest blessed the rope, and the mob tied me to a stake with it. I couldn't get away. They set fire to the sticks under me, chanting that I was a witch, a demon. They had the witch part right, though I never cursed anyone or anything."

"I know. I saw all of it like it was happening to me, Haridan. I can still feel some of it."

"I am sorry that you had to see that. My past isn't the most pleasant of things about me, I assure you."

"No, but you lived it. It's worth someone knowing. Where are you taking the necklace? That's a dangerous fucking piece of jewelry."

"Back to Rome," Haridan said. He fell back onto the bed and dragged his hands down his face with a sigh. "How much do you know about the Romanorum?"

"Other than the occasional customer to my store, I ignore vampires and their politics. Why?"

Timothy slowly circled around the bed as Haridan talked, an admiring look on his face. Jamie scowled at him and muttered, "Leave off, Timothy. You're a ghost, remember?"

"Yeah, but you're not. And this is one prime piece of undead flesh ."

"Shut the fuck up." As right as Timothy might be, Jamie's thoughts weren't really going in that direction. The vampire's life replayed like little bits of film reel in his head. Heading to the other bed, Jamie sat heavily on the edge.

One eyebrow rose, Haridan looking as if he might smile. "Do you two always argue like this? It's rather bizarre to hear you, but not him. What's he saying?"

An aggravated sigh escaped Jamie and he muttered, "Believe me, you don't know to know."

Timothy's grin was unbashed as he stretched out on his side and hovered not too far from Jamie. "I get the first peek at him. Just wait 'til he's naked."

Jamie bite his lower lip to still his outraged protest. He knew Timothy was trying to egg him on and he refused to give the wraith the satisfaction. "I'm sorry, Haridan. Timothy has a habit of butting in."

"I'm sure I've heard worse." Haridan stood and started for the bathroom. "The door is locked. I'm going to take a quick shower." He stripped off his shirt, tossing it onto the bed. A huge raven, wings outstretched, covered his back, the black and silver inkwork so well done, it seemed to move on its own . Then Haridan disappeared into the bathroom.

When Timothy started to follow him, Jamie was almost too distracted by the tattoo to react. The moment Timothy was right behind Haridan, Jamie jumped off the bed, yelling, "Timothy!"

Between gales of laughter, Timothy blurted, "I was only kidding!"

Haridan paused in the doorway and turned, giving Jamie a questioning look. "Dare I ask?"

"He's yanking my chain."

When the door shut behind Haridan, Timothy saw his chance. "No, I wasn't." A split second later, he went through the bathroom door.

Jamie clenched his fists at his sides as he stalked to the door. Should he knock? Damn wraith. He ended up whispering instead. "Timothy, get out here." Getting no response, he lifted his hand, ready to knock, then decided not to. How he could explain why he was knocking? Frustrated, he returned to the bed and threw himself on it, waiting for Haridan to get done.

\* \* \*

Timothy heard the whisper quite well, but in the spirit of driving Jamie crazy, he ignored it. Besides, the vampire really was worth a sneak peek. There was no knowing how long it would take Jamie to check it out for himself. Timothy was only helping him.

Steam fogged up the mirror and Haridan tipped his head back, water pouring down a sculpted body. He was lean, but fit—well toned. His short, auburn hair darkened when wet, and without clothing, the scars on his body stood out, despite the many tattoos. Both nipples were pierced, as was his cock, just on the underside of the head. Haridan soaped his hands and ran them down his chest, over his stomach, then finally down to cup himself before he rinsed.

If he'd have been alive, Timothy would have been drooling. He sure as hell would have never let such a delicious specimen shower alone. Of course, watching only tortured him, and he was more than happy to share the joy. He stuck his head through the door so Jamie could see him. "You are so missing out, bud. This body would stop a Mack truck, and the tattoos..."

"Timothy," Jamie hissed.

The water turned off and the shower curtain opened. Haridan stepped out and grabbed a towel. After drying, he wrapped it around his waist and went back out into the main room. "You're more than welcome to one, too, if you want."

Timothy wouldn't have invaded Haridan's space if he had felt that it would bother the vampire. However, he sensed Haridan was a bit of exhibitionist under the surface and was proven right when Haridan waltzed out in no more than a towel. Timothy followed him and gave Jamie a thumbs up. "You really should have been in there with him. He's got some nice piercings. And that dragon..."

The scowl on Jamie's face seemed to be perpetual. Picking up the nearest item, which happened to be a book on the stand, he threw it at Timothy. Then he got up and stalked into the bathroom.

"I'll tell you more when you get back," Timothy called out cheerfully before the bathroom door slammed shut.

Haridan chuckled and stretched out on one of the beds. "I know you can hear me," he said. "Try speaking to my mind, and by all means, tell me what has him tossing Gideon's Bible across the room."

It took a bit of focus for Timothy to communicate that way since he was used to openly speaking his mind to Jamie. *He knows I watched you in the shower. I didn't think you would mind, but he's not happy with me over it.*

"Ah, so that's why he stormed out. Does he ever loosen up?"

Timothy's teasing nature faded. *"I think your life did a number on him. There's a disquiet in him that isn't normally there. Jamie will loosen up in more ways than one once he adjusts and you get him safely away from here. That's what you're planning on doing, right?"*

Haridan sighed. "Yes. He can't stay here. As much as I imagine he'll fight me on it, I'm taking him to Rome with me. You know who I am, don't you?"

*"Yeah, I do. I recognized the name. I knew there was a reason I trusted you when you came into the store. He'll go with you. I'll make sure of that."*

"I wish I could see him. It takes a lot of energy to focus my magic enough to see him that way, and even then, it's never very clear. He sounds young."

*"He's young, only twenty-two. Not the most knowing, but he's not stupid."* Timothy's humor returned with a vengeance on the subject of appearances. *"Those are some damn fine piercings by the way."*

Haridan grinned. "Thank you. They're quite a bit of fun, too, with the right person."

*"Oh, I already know that. If I had a body, I'd have shown you while you were in the shower."*

Jamie opened the door and when he saw Timothy standing beside Haridan, he just shook his head.

"I see." Haridan paused, head turning in Jamie's direction. A pale blue aura surrounded him for a moment, then he smiled. *"Jesus, he's hot,"* he said silently to Timothy.

Ignoring them both, Jamie pulled down the covers on the other bed. The towel dropped to the floor before he crawled into the bed.

*"It's been torture living with him let me tell you,"* Timothy grumbled.

"I can see why," Haridan muttered.

"See why what?" Jamie asked as he pulled the covers over him.

Clearing his throat, Haridan slid under the covers, tossing his towel onto the floor a second later. "That you're going to be stubborn when we go to Rome," he lied.

"Rome?" Jamie sounded startled, and Timothy intervened before he could say more.

"Yes, Rome. You have to, Jamie. It's not only your life at stake, but Haridan's as well."

"You're going with me," Haridan said. "No arguing." Rolling onto his stomach, he pulled a pillow over his head, muffling a soft growl.

Jamie turned off the light. "Timothy said your life was in danger, too."

"It is," Haridan muttered, flipping back over. "That necklace belongs to my grandfather—Diocourides."

"Your grandfather is Diocourides ? I can't endanger your life over this stupid necklace. I'm sorry I just didn't give it to you right away."

"No harm done, so long as we get to Rome soon." Haridan sat up, the sheet falling to his lap. "I need to leave for a short time."

"Is something wrong?"

"I have to feed. I've gone too long already."

"He's hungry, Jamie," Timothy said. "You know, vampires, blood."

"Blood?" Jamie parroted like an idiot. "You need blood."

"Yes." Haridan growled and patted the bed for his clothes. "Just enough to hold me over until we get to Rome."

"He won't harm you, Jamie. Maybe you should offer. It would be easier than him trying to find somebody else right now. Especially with the laws and all."

Jamie knew Timothy was right. There was no way Haridan could just pick somebody off the street without serious repercussions. The thought really didn't bother Jamie, it was just blood after all. Besides, he might not have fed a vampire himself, but he saw it in the past, usually in dark corners of clubs and always with the donor's consent. Surely it wouldn't be too bad. "Do you know a donor in the city? If not, maybe I can help ?"

"Have you ever fed a vampire?"

"No, I don't know any vampires. But since I'm here and you don't have a donor, I don't think you can be choosy."

Haridan hesitated for a moment, then he sat on the edge beside Jamie. "There is pain, at first, but it fades. Throat or wrist?"

Jamie propped himself on his elbow and offered his wrist to the vampire. His own eyes had adjusted to the darkness, and even though he could barely see Haridan, he knew the vampire didn't need to see him. "I figured it would hurt. After all, you're putting two holes in me."

Haridan took Jamie's hand and brought it to his lips. "Thank you," he whispered. Then he bit down, fangs sinking into Jamie's flesh.

Jamie had prepared himself for the initial sting of pain, expecting it to linger and make this uncomfortable. When the first sliver of pleasurable sensation slid through him, however,

Jamie found himself unable to stop the soft groan. It intensified with each pull of Haridan's mouth, and Jamie began to harden beneath the covers. Dismay, embarrassment at his own reaction, and the heat rapidly flooding his body made him shift restlessly even as he tried to fight it.

Haridan licked the wounds and shuddered as he ran his tongue across his lips, fangs not yet receding. "It's normal. And quite mutual."

Jamie struggled not to show any signs that he'd been affected at all, but the casualness of his voice sounded, even to him, to be a mite strained. "Yeah, it's no big deal. You needed the blood. Was it enough?"

"Yes. Thank you." Haridan got up and headed for the bathroom. "I'll be right back."

Timothy chuckled. "Quite a kicker, isn't it? Why didn't you let him know that you want him?"

A muttered curse was Jamie's only answer. Determinedly, he laid back down and pulled the covers up over his head.

# Chapter Fifteen

They traveled all night, mostly by shadow. Now they had to wait for the plane to come in from Rome. Haridan could make it there if he were alone, but as it was, he had Jamie now to protect. He hadn't planned on any of this, but Haridan figured he might as well make the best of it. Jamie seemed to be strong, despite his young age. The fact that he was attractive didn't help matters, but a perpetual hard-on was a small price to pay if it meant getting the necklace back. So here he stood, in a Romanorum-owned hotel on America's East Coast, trying not to give into urges best left unaddressed.

"So when does this mad dash to safety end?"

"When we reach the safety of Dio's estate. Any idea how Jamie is going to take to living among vampires? He seems to prefer avoiding them. I'm surprised he offered to feed me."

*"He doesn't know anything about them, other than minor basics,"* Timothy said. *"He always avoided any major vamp hang outs, but he doesn't avoid vampires, per se. Just the scene. Working like he does, he's just never come into any direct contact outside of the occasional customer."*

Haridan sat down on the edge of the single king-size bed and expended a bit of energy to look at Jamie. He didn't need to get involved, but he couldn't help the unexplainable draw he felt toward the young man. He reached out and brushed a bit of hair from Jamie's forehead, then smoothed his fingers over the man's cheek. "If I'm not careful..."

*"He's a clueless kid in a lot of ways. Just remember that when you're dealing with him."* There was a pause before Timothy

added, *"Getting attached? That's not necessarily a bad thing. It's easy to get attached to him. Just don't fuck him up, Haridan."*

"I doubt he'd want to get involved with me anyway. I've taken him from life as he knew it. But I'd be lying if I said I didn't want him."

*"With Jamie, it's always hard telling. Hell, if I were living, you'd be pinning me to the bed. Know any magic that lets a ghost have a bit of fun?"*

That surprised a laugh out of Haridan. "Nothing permanent, but I have a few tricks up my sleeve."

*"I'm wondering if I should take you up on that."*

Jamie stirred, beginning to wake up. When he opened his eyes, he saw Haridan staring at him. "What time is it?"

"I'd be happy to try, Timothy," Haridan answered. "And it's seven in the evening. Are you hungry?"

"Yeah, I am." Jamie sat up and rubbed his eyes. "You're talking to Timothy?"

"I am. In a sense. He's mindspeaking." Haridan tried to ignore the fact that Jamie was so close. He let the spell fade that had allowed him temporary sight. "What would you like?"

"Probably should just order a hamburger from room service."

Haridan felt the bed shift when Jamie sat up and he licked his lips. He might've been blind, but his sense of smell was strong. Jamie's natural scent filled Haridan, and beneath it, the faintest hint of Jamie's blood, flowing steadily within him. It took all the control Haridan had to keep from taking what he wanted.

"You'll have to order," he said finally. "No braille phones here."

*"Easy there,"* Timothy whispered to Haridan. *"The boy is as dense as a brick."*

"Give me a second to wake up and I will." The bed dipped for a second and then Jamie picked up the phone. "When are we supposed to leave here?"

"When they call to tell us the plane has landed. Tonight or tomorrow night."

"Oh, hi. I'd like to order a hamburger and fries on the side." Jamie paused for a moment, then continued. "No, no salad, but I'll take a Pepsi. Thanks." Jamie hung up the phone and yawned. "We going to stay in the hotel room? How far do you think those guys might be able to track us?"

"I don't know," Haridan said. "They aren't working alone. Hell, they're working for someone else, though I don't know who yet."

"Won't they lay off once Diocourides has the necklace back? And am I going to stay in Rome, or are you guys going to kill me?"

Haridan, who'd been pacing, spun around, and blurted out the first thing that came to mind. "Kill you? You're more in danger of me fucking you than you are dying at our hands."

"What reason is there for letting me live?" Jamie asked quietly.

Haridan sighed. "We aren't going to kill you. None of this is your fault in any way.

"I know it's not my fault, but there's no logical reason to let me live, is there?"

Haridan grumbled and crouched down in Jamie's general vicinity. "Listen. You've done nothing wrong. Now, if you were to take what you know about me—about my life and my weakness—and use it against me. Then you'd be in trouble. But honestly, I don't see you doing that. Dio will welcome you."

"No, I wouldn't do that, but you only have my word. Is Diocourides going to take me in and provide for me for the rest of my life? I clearly can't go out and get a job if some insane vampires are after me."

"There are many positions for mortals within his court. And if you ever found a vampire to whom you wish to bond, you have the option of becoming a ghoul—bound to that vampire forever. It's not a thing to enter into lightly, but the choice is there should you ever reach that point. I will do anything I can to help ease the transition into court life, if you'll let me."

Silence filled the space between them for a moment, then Jamie cleared his throat. "I trust you. I know that sounds weird, considering we just met, but I know I feel comfortable around you. Never thought about the fact that you might not be around after this. Would you bond with me?"

Out of all the things Haridan had expected, that question sure as hell wasn't one of them. "I..." He raked a hand through his hair, brow furrowed. "God, Jamies. It would be a lie if I said I didn't want to, but I won't do it without you knowing what to expect."

Jamie sighed. "If I go to Rome, I'm going to be surrounded by others I don't even know. Definitely in closer quarters than a city would be. Like I said, I trust you. You're the only one I know, and I know you far better than I will ever know any other person on this earth. Does that make sense to you?"

"Yeah. Yeah, it does. You've seen my life, you know the stories behind the scars, behind how I became the man I am."

Haridan rose up and sat on the bed beside Jamie. "Once it is done, it cannot be undone . Are you sure you want this?"

"I've heard one or two things about vampire society. I don't know if it's true, but if mortals are considered free territory, then yeah, I am."

"As my ghoul, you will have my blood within you," Haridan explained. "Vampires and other ghouls will know you are bound to me and thus, you will be off-limits. Are you aware that it requires drinking my blood frequently? I wouldn't recommend more than two days without. Seven, and it will begin to drive you insane until you have it. Your senses will be more acute, and you'll know my thoughts and I yours, unless I close off the contact."

"You mean I'll have to drink your blood for the rest of my life?"

"Yes. From the first drop, it will become a craving."

"My folks are dead, no siblings—not like anyone will really miss me anyway. I think I can handle that. I'm stuck in your world , and I'd like to be safe in it."

"You will be. That I promise you." Haridan thought for a moment, then asked, "Do you wish to drink from my wrist or my throat?"

The bed shifted when Jamie slipped down to kneel at Haridan's feet. "Your wrist, I guess."

Haridan swallowed, acutely aware that Jamie was right there, within easy reach and at the perfect level for something much different. "As you wish," he whispered, his voice a bit rough. He bit down on his wrist, then offered it to Jamie. "Drink."

* * *

At the sight of the blood welling from the wound, Jamie had a moment of squeamishness, but he swallowed it down quickly. His options were too limited in this. He reached for Haridan's wrist and drew it hesitantly to his lips. His tongue darted out to take an experimental taste and he found the odd, slightly coppery taste not as bad as he thought. As he fastened his mouth to the cut, a sudden need surged though him. Without giving himself more time to think, he began to drink, mouth hungrily pulling in as much blood as he could get.

Haridan groaned, shifting on the bed. With his other hand, he cupped the back of Jamie's head, fingers flexing in Jamie's hair. "Fuck," he hissed.

When he felt he'd had enough and the strange need faded, Jamie released Haridan. He remained where he knelt, though, dazed by what had just happened. He tasted the vampire's blood on his tongue, his lips; felt it coursing through his veins. The sensations sent a shiver through him, followed swiftly by desire so strong, he could barely contain it.

Haridan opened and closed his fingers, digging his nails into his palms. Then he fell backward onto the bed, letting out a slow exhale. "Jesus."

"Are you okay?"

"I'm fine," Haridan muttered, voice raw.

"Have you ever done this before? Do you have any others who drink your blood?" As odd as his own reaction had been, Jamie wondered if Haridan felt the same.

"No. Aside from my Father, the one who turned me, I've never felt that."

Jamie smiled. In a way, it made him feel somewhat unique since he knew Haridan was over a thousand years old. "That's kind of a relief. To me, anyway."

Haridan sat up and winced. He dropped back down with a grunt. "Excuse me for a second," he muttered as he shifted himself in his jeans.

Jamie tried not to notice while Timothy burst out laughing. It was clear to Jamie that he'd aroused the vampire, and he wasn't quite sure how to react himself. Would it always be like this? Thankfully, a knock at the door saved him. Hastily scrambling to his feet, he went to the door and opened it. When he saw the hotel clerk holding a tray, he took it, and thanked the man before closing the door again.

When Jamie turned around again, Haridan was walking into the bathroom. "I'll be right out," the vampire said before closing the door between them.

# Chapter Sixteen

*Five days later...*

Diocourides' home was like nothing Jamie had ever seen. The palazio was a harmonious blending of old and new. Two flights of stairs led to the upper level entry of the house, the ancient stone varying from gray to black to white. The bottom level held a multitude of windows on each side of a huge entry way of glass and wood, and the second floor displayed the same pattern of windows. When they arrived, Haridan took Jamie to a private, third floor wing. Jamie had his own set of rooms, which he found weird. His sitting room, as Haridan called it, was big enough to hold his old apartment in its entirety.

His bedroom had its own fireplace and a red-canopied bed took center stage. The canopy hung from the ceiling and surrounded the bed with deep red velvet draperies. Small, antique scenery paintings lined one of the walls, and a huge, dark wood armoire took up almost the length of another wall, along with an ornate writing desk. It hadn't taken Jamie long to settle in since he didn't have anything with him but the clothes on his back.

Because he could see ghosts, Jamie could tell the difference between the vampires and ghouls. He could tell just from attitude alone who was important, or at least those who thought they were. Since he hadn't been introduced to Diocourides yet, he wasn't officially part of the circle, and he wasn't sure he wanted to be. From what he'd seen just in the first moments of his arrival, there was a distinct hierarchy that left him feeling more than a bit of out of place.

Haridan had already disappeared a few times, but instead of hiding, Jamie chose to explore his new home. The entire first floor and gardens were the public rooms. At any given time, day or night, there were people either waiting to see Diocourides or enjoying inner circle politics. Haridan had told him that the second floor housed all the business offices of the Romanorum. He also knew Diocourides' rooms were across the hall from Haridan's, but he'd yet to see the elusive elder vampire.

Pretty much everywhere Jamie went, he was ignored, and it didn't bother him. He tended to be out of place in his casual clothes, but the higher echelon chose not to notice him. Either the others had been told to leave him alone or they genuinely decided not to give a damn. Jamie figured it was a combination of the two.

He headed down the back stairs to the servants' dining rooms. Even with the mortals and ghouls, there was some kind of 'I'm better than you' structure. Those who served more powerful vampires dined in the rooms furthest from the kitchens. Household servants and more low-status ghouls ate either in the kitchen or in one of the rooms beside it. Since Jamie had no clue where he was supposed to be, and couldn't care less anyway, he went for the kitchen. The appetizing aromas filled the hall and dining rooms, and made Jamie's stomach rumble as he helped himself to slices of roast chicken, pasta, and corn. Everything was laid out on a buffet style table, and it appeared to be an all you can eat, serve yourself.

"You're Haridan's, aren't you?"

Jamie sat at one of the tables. "Yeah, why?"

"Just curious. We heard he'd taken on an outsider. So how come you're in here and not in the main dining room?"

"'Cuz I want to be in here." Jamie casually eyed the blond guy talking to him. On a scale of one to ten, the man rated a decent seven. He was damn good looking in a rough, biker type way—something Jamie hadn't expected to see.

"Well, you're sitting with the bottom of the food chain. I'm Eddie, and the ice blond goddess is Ingrid. The Irish redhead is Tommy, and the sawed-off Russian is Vladimir."

"Bottom of the food chain?"

The other three stared at Jamie. Eddie shrugged. "You haven't hung around vamps much, have you? We're donors. Freelance. It's a fairly cushy job, even if we are at the bottom."

"I haven't the first clue about any of this." Jamie ate his food. There was a definite pecking order, starting with the tables closest to the door—he could feel it.

"You lucked in, Jamie. Haridan is one of Diocourides' grandkids. He has the ear of the inner circle. Not all the vamps are keen on being nice to their cows, but Dio makes sure they behave. They all have to be decent to you. Or risk pissing off not only Dio, but Haridan, too."

"How in the hell can you tell who is who?"

Ingrid blinked at Jamie in disbelief. "You don't know shit, do you?"

"Vampires weren't any part of my life until recently."

"The others are going to have fun with you." Eddie remarked, showing a bit of sympathy.

Tommy kindly filled Jamie in. "The older vamps and ghouls will know who you are by Haridan's signature on your chest. Younger ones might not figure it out, but if they screw up, they'll find out quickly enough. There's a whole world of rules, and this is the heart of the Romanorum. Even at the bottom of the chain, this is one hell of a place to live."

As the three got up, Jamie followed them, carrying his dishes to an inset window between the room and kitchen.

"You can stay with us if you want. At least you'll learn something, and we'll benefit from the prestige." Ingrid flashed him a grin as she slapped him on the back.

Walking down the corridor, Eddie pointed out each room and its occupants. "After the freelancers, the rooms go by formula. Sixth has the two closest to the ones we eat in. Then fifth, fourth, third, second, and of course, first. Which is where you're supposed to eat."

Jamie noticed the rooms were exactly identical except for their position in the hall. Each had several long tables lined with dining chairs. There were no special decorations in the rooms, other than the same painted murals above the wood paneling of the walls. Jamie eyed the ghouls in the first formula dining room. There were only a few there, and a couple of them looked askance at Jamie when they noticed who he was with. Tommy gave them a swaggering wave and Ingrid blew them a kiss.

Shaking his head, Jamie laughed before Eddie continued down the hall. "We're heading for the central meeting room," Eddie explained. "It's where everybody congregates to get Dio to listen to their complaints."

"Not all the ghouls are stuffed shirts. Some are pretty decent. It really depends on their master. Quite a few of the vampires are very conscious of their status. Dio discourages it, but they don't always listen to him about that," Vladimir said, his Russian accent thick. It was stronger than Tommy and

Ingrid's accents. Most likely he hadn't been there as long as the other two. Eddie's tone had a thick Southern twang, so clearly he was fairly new as well.

"You'll see it all in action in the session," Eddie said. "We don't have to attend unless required, but it's a good place to figure it all out."

A vampire stood near the entry of the throne room and greeted them all by name. Jamie eyed him in curiosity as the others returned the greeting.

"D is the one who can tell you the most about this place." Eddie flashed Jamie a grin. "He's been here the longest ."

"Taking the new one under your wing, Eddie?" the vampire asked.

"Somebody has to before the sharks decide to play with him."

"I doubt they'd get too far. Jamie seems pretty level-headed."

While D might have been there for a long time, he didn't even look to be of legal age. He couldn't have been eighteen. Sixteen, maybe, but no older than that. Floored, Jamie stared at him. With some vampires, their years were still visible in their eyes. A sense of agelessness, world weariness, or just having seen too much. D's blue eyes were bright and shiny, undimmed by any sign of age whatsoever. For some reason, D seemed familiar to Jamie. It took him a moment to remember he'd seen D in some of Haridan's memories.

"I know you from what I saw of Haridan's past."

"Yes, the necklace. I know." D dismissed the others with a slight gesture. "My grandson told me what happened."

"Grandson?" Jamie blinked, unable to look away from D. When the realization hit, he felt like an idiot for not catching on sooner. This was Diocourides? "Nobody told me you looked this young. You're a kid."

A smile quirked the corner of Dio's lips. "I was seventy when I died. That was a couple of thousand years ago. Nobody said I couldn't be vain about something. It's why I've used magic to keep myself looking this young."

"You're not even legal in the States." Since he knew a great many of Haridan's memories of Dio were either humorous or sentimental, Jamie actually found it hard to view the vampire with any fear.

"Only some have reason to be afraid of me, Jamie, and you're not one of them."

When the crowd fell silent, Jamie remained at the back of the room. Dio headed to the carved and decorated dais that held a single throne. A wooden canopy covered the ceiling just above the chair. To Jamie, it looked like a regular arm chair and definitely didn't fit the ornate setting around it. Instead of sitting on it, Dio chose to sit on the top step of the dais.

"He's a hell of a lot different than what I expected," Timothy said, appearing beside Jamie.

"No shit." Jamie scanned the growing crowd for Haridan. He hadn't seen the vampire in a few days, since just after they'd arrived. When he spotted him, Jamie edged his way through the room toward Haridan. Because of that necklace, Jamie knew Haridan in ways he'd never known another. Haridan's life had been laid out before Jamie as if he'd lived it. The entire experience had brought Jamie closer to Haridan, though he hadn't realized it at first. It wasn't just about wanting Haridan's blood.

The remote, stern lines of Haridan's face kept the others away from him. Jamie ignored the expression as he took his place beside the vampire. Haridan didn't even seem aware of him, and Jamie sighed inwardly.

# Chapter Seventeen

Jamie heard voices and the soft strains of music as he listened near the closed door. He dressed in a suit that didn't quite sit well with him, but he'd given into the idea when Haridan had brought it to his room. The whole outfit had an old-fashioned look, reminding him of something he'd seen in a history book. The severe black was relieved only by the glittering emerald pin in what Jamie thought passed for a tie.

Suppressing a sigh, he opened the door and stepped inside. Unlike his imagination, the voices didn't still, nor did the room fall into complete silence, but he was aware of a great many eyes on him. He ignored everybody as he looked desperately around for Haridan while still trying to appear calm. Jamie spotted Diocourides standing with a group of others, and tried to walk over to the vampire as composedly as he could.

The door opened a moment later and Haridan walked out, laughing at something a fellow vampire had said. Dressed in his usual dark jeans and T-shirt, a black trench coat over it all, he looked a bit out of place amid the finery of the others in the room. His black sunglasses hid his eyes. He stopped in front of Jamie and smiled. "Even spells are not perfect, but from what I can see with it, you look good."

Jamie's gaze narrowed on the casual attire Haridan sported. "Now tell me why I'm wearing this if you can wear jeans." He caught the smile twitching at Dio's lips and included the other vampire in his disgruntled stare.

Haridan laughed. "Because my Grandfather knows I'll buck tradition no matter what he does or says."

"Do not encourage him, Samuel," Dio said to Haridan, the glint in his eyes reflecting his good humor. "The others have been patiently waiting for you to arrive."

Jamie stepped closer to Haridan when he become the focus of everybody's attention. Haridan put his arm around Jamie's shoulders. Leaning down, he whispered in Jamie's ear, "Believe me, it amuses him."

Jamie nestled to Haridan's side as Dio turned to face the others and raised his voice. "Tonight, I am officially announcing an addition to my family. My grandson, Samuel Haridan, has chosen Jamie as his companion and given Jamie the blood of our line." Dio held out his hand to Jamie. "Welcome to our family."

Grateful for the kindness of Dio's words, Jamie took the elder vampire's hand, clasping it lightly. "Thank you, Diocourides."

Haridan stepped behind Jamie, arms sliding around Jamie's waist. "As you show me respect and kindness," he said to the court, "I expect you all to show the same to him."

The others around them bowed their heads politely. From what Jamie had learned thus far, it was highly doubtful any of the court would object to anything that already had Diocourides' approval. A few of the members regarded Jamie with a friendly eye; the others paid him relatively little attention for more than a brief moment. With a wave of Dio's hand, they all drifted off, leaving them the three of them alone.

Once he ceased to be the center of attention, Jamie's tension eased completely. "Thank you as well, Haridan. Without you, I doubt the others would be so nice."

"My pleasure," Haridan said. "Are you hungry?"

"Actually, yes."

"The others are in the dining hall," Dio suggested. "Why don't you go join them? The cooks have prepared a special feast for your introduction to the family."

Jamie nodded. "I'll get something to eat and head back to my room."

"I'll join you soon."

* * *

Dio tucked his hand under Haridan's arm. "Shall we talk in my sanctuary or in the gardens?"

Haridan slipped off his glasses and rubbed his eyes with his free hand. "Gardens. I'd like the fresh air."

"We'll just leave the others to amuse themselves." Dio lead Haridan outside into the quiet of the garden.

Haridan took a deep breath. "It's nice to be home."

"I know you had a hard time retrieving the necklace, Samuel. I never thought it would surface. It will take me time to prepare what I need to destroy it, but I will destroy it myself this time."

"Good. Jamie touched it before I could stop him."

Dio paused, his fingers tightening slightly on Haridan's arm. "I can feel you've been troubled lately. It has to do with Jamie, doesn't it? Does he even realize what you choosing him as your companion means?"

"I don't think he knows how I feel," Haridan said quietly. "I know he's attracted to me, but for some reason, he avoids any contact."

"Samuel, you have to remember he has a lot to deal with here. His life is now far different from what it was. It will take him time to adjust. Since he touched the necklace, he knows you as well as I know you. He's also comfortable with me now. I'm impressed he shows such a great ability to adapt."

"I know. I never meant to drag him into this, but I couldn't leave him to die. It's not in me—you know that." He sighed and raked a hand through his hair. "I just didn't intend to fall, either."

"I would have expected you to bring him here, so I won't fault you for your decision. I trust your instincts as well. For some reason, you've chosen this mortal for your own, and you can't control your own feelings all of the time. No matter that you try so hard," Dio chuckled.

"I was perfectly content to stand alone," Haridan muttered, though he wondered if he even believed that anymore. He had a damn good feeling Dio didn't. Then again, Dio could see through him like he was made of glass.

"You *thought* you were content. There is a difference, Child. At least the occasional nonsense of someone taking it into their heads to try to pursue you will end. Not that it wasn't entertaining at times, but I'd rather see you happy." Dio lightly patted Haridan's cheek in an affectionate gesture. "After accepting Joshua as my own, I have quite often dearly hoped the same for you."

Haridan laughed. "Point taken."

"I do expect a bit of grumbling from one or two of the others, but I don't believe they'll say anything openly to me or you. I'm thinking, particularly, of Cam and Octavia. You'll want to keep an eye on them."

"Cam finally got the hint the last time he tried cornering me in the hall," Haridan grumbled. "Octavia is a little more...stubborn."

"There is prestige attached to your name, something I think doesn't impress your Jamie all that much." As they continued their walk in the garden, a light breeze carried the sweet perfume of the blooming roses. "And I've seen the wraith who follows him around. He's an amusing fellow when he doesn't realize he's being watched."

"Timothy is entertaining." Haridan stopped for a moment. "What does Jamie look like? My magic doesn't make things brilliantly clear. I wish I could see him better."

"Timothy talks about you often. Jamie has all of the youthful appearance of his young age. His eyes are green, darker in hue than grass. More the color of dense forest growth in the shadows. His hair is about shoulder-length and black, fairly straight. He's built more along the lines of my own body, slender but not overly so."

"One of these days, maybe I'll feel it for myself." Haridan grimaced. "What has Timothy said?"

"The ghost seems to love teasing Jamie about you. He also follows you around sometimes. Eventually I will have to tell them I can see him." Dio's laughter had a teasing edge to it. "You have a very long time to get to know Jamie. It's not likely he'll be able to resist you for long."

"I hope not. The kid's gonna give me blue balls." A servant nearby gasped, but Haridan ignored her. It was no secret how he spoke to Dio in private.

The sound of Dio's laughter rang out in the garden. "You are suffering. I feel for you, I really do."

"Sure you do."

"All right, I don't. But the situation is something I know you're not used to. Allow me to enjoy it."

"Yeah, yeah. You, at least, have Joshua to alleviate your...pains," Haridan said.

# Chapter Eighteen

Haridan leaned on the railing, eyes closed. He couldn't deny it any longer. The more time went by, the more he realized he'd fallen head over heels for the young man he'd taken under his wing. Finally figuring he'd waited long enough, he left the balcony and went back into his room, intent on finding Jamie and declaring what he felt. He'd been keeping it inside for too long and if he didn't say something soon, he was going to go insane. He stepped out of his room and turned right, heading toward the darker end of the hall and the lone entrance that led out to the courtyard. No doubt, Jamie was somewhere with Dio, privy to all manner of stories Haridan wasn't sure he wanted the man to hear.

The moment he stepped into the courtyard, choking darkness engulfed him without warning. Before Haridan could react, his hands were bound with rope and tied with expert ease behind his back. The burning started immediately, the pain bolting through his body. He tried to struggle and almost shouted, but the press of a razor-sharp blade to his throat stopped him cold. His skin burned, the stench of charred flesh strong. He didn't dare move a muscle. Weakness began setting in quickly, the poison on the ropes seeping into his body.

"Get him out of here," a male voice hissed softly.

The blade remained at his throat until he was shoved forward deeper into the shadows. A second later the darkness faded and Haridan expended a minute bit of energy to get his bearings. He was in a bare room with no windows and only one door, but where exactly, he had no idea. A hand roughly shoved him to the ground.

"Now, let's just wait here all cozy-like until my master gets what he wants."

The door opened and someone entered the room. Shaking his head to clear the haze of pain from it, Haridan looked up, the spell holding just enough for him to see the faintest details. Shock froze him where he knelt. It had been years—centuries—since he'd seen his cousin, but Aldrich hadn't changed a damn bit. He was still the arrogant, ruthless bastard he always had been, just like his damned Father. Dark hair held at the nape of his neck, his long coat brushing the dirty stone floor, Aldrich even moved like Triarius—stalking, purposeful. But there was more malice in those eyes than Haridan ever remembered seeing before. Aldrich crouched down and snagged a handful of hair, yanking Haridan's head back at a painful angle.

"What the fuck do you want?" Haridan snarled.

"Emery is delivering the message as we speak, Aldrich," one of the others said. "It shouldn't be too long."

"Nice to see you too, cousin. I won't be keeping you long, so just relax." Glancing over at his man, Aldrich's express became more sour. His voice was harsh, and he didn't seem all that forgiving. "At least you made up for the mess you made at that American store."

"You," Haridan growled. "You're behind this shit?"

The other vampire shifted a little. "Yes, Aldrich, sir."

"Fucking arse." Aldrich dismissed him, turning his attention back to Haridan. He jerked Haridan's head back again before he finally let him go. His lips twisted as he eyed

Haridan in disdain. "It's about time you're worth something in your life, cousin. I'm pretty sure the old man won't let anything harm you."

Haridan scowled, then winced, the burn from the ropes spreading up his arms. "Your fucking Father put you up to this?"

Aldrich snorted as he straightened from his position. "He's too bloody weak to do anything. Triarius thinks more of his pleasure now than who we are." Walking slowly behind Haridan, he examined the ropes cutting into Haridan's flesh. "Don't think you can handle too much more of this, can you?"

"You *know* I can't," Haridan shot back. "He doesn't know you're here, does he?" Fuck, if Triarius hadn't initiated this, then there was yet more trouble ahead. Unlike his Father, who had mellowed somewhat, according to Dio, Aldrich saw nothing but dominance over the Romanorum. That explained why Aldrich needed the necklace. "What are you going to do?"

Aldrich grabbed the rope and yanked it, wrenching Haridan's arms backward painfully, before he stepped back to the front. "Get rid of you, your grandfather, and anybody else who opposes me. What the fucking else do you think I'm going to?"

"The message was delivered, Aldrich," someone to the side said. "It's time to alert the others."

Haridan, still reeling from the shock of intense pain, dropped to the floor. Jamie. Fuck, he had to get to Jamie. Where the fuck was he? Panting, his wrists on fire, he closed his eyes and willed himself to think clearly as he fought the urge to give into the poison coursing through his veins at lightning speed.

"Take care of it, Garrick." Aldrich barked out his orders, taking hold of Haridan's arm and dragging him to his feet. "Emery, you know what to do."

The others left the room, and a moment later Aldrich pulled Haridan with him into nearby shadows, heedless of any pain Haridan felt. After very little time in the darkness, they emerged into a huge, rundown warehouse. The entire room was filled with broken crates and rusted machinery. Haridan struggled to keep the spell up, though it was quickly losing strength. How Aldrich knew about his weakness, Haridan didn't know, but he prayed Dio would send someone soon. Dying here, in the middle of nowhere, wasn't on Haridan's list of priorities.

The vampire called Emery arrived just in time as Diocourides suddenly appeared in the open doorway leading to the outside of the building. The elder vampire lifted his hand, dangling the delicate pearl necklace from his fingers. Haridan jerked away from Aldrich, every muscle tense. Dio wasn't stupid—the man had a plan for everything, and Haridan prayed this time was no exception. Dio's expression one of quiet resolve. Emery took the necklace and slipped it around his neck.

"Just for safe keeping," Emery said, tapping it where it lay against the hollow of his throat.

"Emery!" Infuriated, Aldrich charged forward, his features twisted in rage. Before he could get close, Emery's high-pitched scream echoed in the cavernous room. The vampire fell to the floor, desperately clawing at himself, but Haridan couldn't see what was wrong. Without waiting for anymore, Aldrich instantly disappeared, leaving his man to thrash and shriek.

Haridan hit the floor, the sounds of the vampire's slow death and the stench of melting flesh enough to make him retch. Arms still bound behind him, he fell forward, strong arms catching him. He inhaled deeply, breathing in Dio's scent as the man gently removed the ropes.

"Haridan."

"I'm..." Haridan shuddered. "Just get me home."

* * *

"I wonder where Haridan is?" Jamie leaned over the railing of the balcony. The garden below was lit and others were gathered outside, enjoy the night air. He could see Diocourides standing beside several vampires he didn't recognize. "There must be a new delegation here."

Timothy drifted to stand beside him. "I think Haridan will show up sooner or later."

The first three weeks Jamie had spent in this palatial estate, he'd followed Haridan like a little lost puppy. Maybe the poor guy had just needed a break from him. It hadn't been easy at first to become comfortable around everybody. Jamie was grateful he was housed in Diocourides' personal wing. He really didn't have to mingle with the others unless he wanted to.

"Why don't you just admit it?" Timothy asked him.

"Admit what?"

"That you miss him. That you want him."

"I know I miss him." Jamie turned toward the spirit, resting his elbow on the rail. "There are people here who probably interest him a lot more than me. So why admit to something stupid like that?"

"You've got to be kidding," Timothy said dryly. "Jamie, he watches you when you sleep. He whispers your name when he jerks off after either of you feed."

"You've been watching him!" Aghast, Jamie scowled at Timothy. "You can't do that, damn it!"

"What? He's lonely. He wants you, but for some reason, you won't get near him except to feed. Besides, he's hot."

"I wasn't sure how I felt about him." Jamie pushed off the railing and went back into the bedroom. "It's been a lot to get used to. You think he might be tired of me? Is that why he disappeared earlier tonight without saying anything?" The question was asked with a painful clarity that Haridan might have tired of Jamie not wanting to get too close.

"Why don't you ask him?" Timothy asked, looking at something over Jamie's shoulder.

Jamie turned and saw Haridan in the doorway. Clothes dirty, face haggard, the vampire looked... Well, like he'd been through Hell. Jamie rushed over.

"Are you all right?"

"I am now," Haridan said, giving him a weak smile. "I need a shower."

"What happened? You look terrible."

Realizing he probably shouldn't hold Haridan up, given the man was much bigger, Jamie stepped back a little, but still helped Haridan to the bathroom. The moment Haridan fell in the doorway, Jamie dropped to the floor with him. He grabbed Haridan's hand and saw the edge of the burn beneath the vampire's cuff. It was raw and definitely not healing.

"You need blood. Why didn't you tell me?"

Not letting Haridan argue, Jamie helped him into a sitting position, then knelt in front of him. As he tilted his head, he lifted his hand and took hold of Haridan's head, drawing it to his throat.

"Jamie..." Haridan bit down, fangs sinking deep. He shuddered and pressed closer, biting harder.

Leaning into Haridan, Jamie held on as he let the man feed. He was still pissed Haridan hadn't told him, but he was more concerned with helping. Trying to keep his mind on the task, he tried to ignore the reactions of his body to Haridan's closeness. There were more important issues and questions at hand.

"Just drink, Haridan."

Haridan continued for several more minutes, then licked the wounds before resting his head to Jamie's shoulder. "I needed you," he whispered. "I could see you in my mind, smell your blood, feel you. I just wanted to come home."

"I thought maybe you got tired of me. Let's get you cleaned up and comfortable." Whatever the hell had happened to Haridan, he hadn't left by choice. That much was certain. Jamie stood and helped Haridan up and into the bathroom.

Haridan leaned against the door frame while Jamie got the water going. "They didn't tell you because they didn't want you to worry. There's no way in hell I'd ever get tired of you."

"I just thought three weeks of me following you around everywhere might have been a bit much for you." Turning back to Haridan, Jamie helped to get his shirt off and tossed it to the floor. The marks on Haridan's wrists weren't as raw as they had been. They looked distinctly like rope burns. "Why did somebody tie you up?"

"They found it amusing to hold Dio's grandson for ransom." Haridan toed off his boots and unfastened his jeans. He stripped out of them, then tossed them to the side. "Being royalty can suck sometimes."

# Chapter Nineteen

When Haridan was undressed, Jamie got the tub filled and helped him into it. As Haridan settled , Jamie grabbed the liquid soap and lathered a wash cloth. "I think that means you need more body guards when you leave this place."

Haridan chuckled. "Dio said the same thing."

"He's a very wise man. So listen to him." Jamie began washing Haridan's chest, silently congratulating himself on keeping his lustful reflections subdued. It was rather difficult, though, when running his hand over the muscular planes of Haridan's skin, but he was trying, damn it.

Haridan caught Jamie's hand. "I don't have to see you to know what's going through your mind," he said quietly.

Jamie didn't say anything for a long moment as he stared down at Haridan's hand over his. "I'm trying to keep it low key."

"Why?"

"I guess until we can really have a chance to talk. Maybe after your bath and a good night's rest. You need both."

"I need you," Haridan said. "I've needed you since the first night I fed from you."

"I've felt that sometimes, but I wasn't sure if it was you or just my own wishful thinking." Jamie slowly continued to wash Haridan, his gaze roaming freely over the vampire's body. "The last few weeks have shown me how much I need you."

Haridan reached up, brushing his fingertips over Jamie's lips. "Believe me, I want you, Jamie. Every waking moment, I have to stop myself from touching you."

"You wouldn't be the only one with that problem."

"Come here." Haridan slipped his hand back, cupping Jamie's head.

With no hesitation, Jamie leaned forward and kissed him. It was something he'd wanted to do a few days after he met Haridan. The touch of Haridan's lips to his sent an instant reaction rushing through his body. Haridan licked Jamie's lips, then parted them with his tongue, humming into the kiss.

"I am yours, Jamie," the vampire murmured. "I have been since the first time I tasted you."

"Is that what bonding means?" Jamie drew back and resumed washing Haridan before he handed the washcloth over to let Haridan finish. "Maybe you should finish up so we can talk about this more comfortably."

"Yes and no. Every person tastes different—blood, semen, you name it—and from the moment I first tasted you, I wanted more than I thought you'd be willing to give." Haridan took the washcloth and washed the last of the dried blood from his skin, rising up on his knees to do so.

When Jamie saw the piercings, he shifted position, suddenly uncomfortable in his jeans. Timothy had teased him unmercifully about Haridan's piercings, and now he saw why. Intriguing was a poor word. Jamie settled back on his feet, blatantly watching the motion of Haridan's hand and the washcloth.

"This isn't the only one," Haridan said, flicking the ring on the underside of his cock. "I have another, in addition to my nipples."

"Guess that means I have to play find the piercing."

Haridan grinned and spread his arms out to the side. "Have at it."

"I think it's time to get out of the bathtub," Jamie laughed. He stood and walked back into Haridan's bedroom, figuring it wouldn't take the vampire long to get his ass out.

Within a few seconds, Haridan was on the bed, shadows receding into nothingness. He stretched out, one arm behind his head, the other hand resting on his stomach, just above his towel. Jamie shook his head and grinned. He crawled onto the bed and settled beside Haridan.

"Are you still curious where the other one is?" Haridan asked.

In answer, Jamie shifted close enough to begin his own exploration with hands and tongue. He ran one hand over the smooth flesh of Haridan's stomach and his lower body pressed against Haridan's thigh, giving his hardening cock a bit of friction that aroused him even more. Haridan tasted like soap and musk, his scent strong. Beneath it all, Jamie breathed in the hint of the vampire's blood, the smell alone enough to make him ache.

Haridan groaned, stomach muscles tightening beneath Jamie's touch. "Jamie..."

He wanted to take his time, to learn every inch of this man who'd stolen him from life as he knew it. Jamie licked and nipped his way down Haridan's body until he reached the vampire's cock. The ring there, just below the head, beckoned him and Jamie gave in, catching the steel loop with his teeth. Haridan hissed, hands landing on Jamie's head, fingers tugging but not pulling him away. Jamie flicked the ring with his tongue, then slipped his lips over the head of Haridan's cock.

"Jamie!" Haridan bucked, his hold tight in Jamie's hair.

Encouraged, Jamie sucked the vampire down, the sensation of the ring on his tongue not as odd as he'd thought it would be. He cupped Haridan's balls and that's when he felt it—the second ring. He groaned, the sound muffled, and pulled gently on the ring. Haridan jerked beneath him, the vampire's legs spreading in invitation. Jamie hummed and bobbed his head up and down, eyes closing as he focused on the musky taste, the feel of smooth skin broken only by warm steel.

"J-Jamie..." Haridan moaned and rolled his hips upward. "Ride me."

Although he was reluctant to stop, the thought of this thickness inside him spurred Jamie to move. He pulled off with a final lick and smiled when Haridan grunted. "Lube?"

Haridan pointed to the side, presumably to the bedside table, though his aim was a bit off. "Table drawer. Hurry."

Jamie laughed and crawled up and over Haridan, straddling the man's waist while he reached for the table. Warm, wet heat covered his left nipple without warning and Jamie damn near collapsed, the touch of Haridan's tongue maddening. "You're not helping," he muttered.

"Oops." Haridan sounded completely unrepentant, but he dropped his head back down on the pillow and licked his lips. "By all means..." He thrust up, cock sliding along Jamie's ass.

"Yeah," Jamie said, breathlessly. He grabbed the lube out of the table and lifted up. Sitting back a little, he held the bottle over Haridan and grinned when the vampire hissed at the cool gel on his heated skin. Snapping the bottle closed, Jamie fisted Haridan's cock and stroked, earning himself a deep-seated growl.

"Jamie."

Jamie slid up and reached back, lined Haridan up, then sank down. "Oh, sweet fuck..." The ring in Haridan's prick grazed him inside, slick and smooth, and dear God... "Haridan."

Haridan gripped Jamie's hips and held him down as he thrust up. Jamie shouted, throwing his head back as Haridan nailed his gland. "Yes. Ride me, Jamie."

The entire world tilted and Jamie could only hold on, fingers digging into the vampire's chest as he started grinding and rocking, lifting and falling with Haridan's help. Every stroke sent sparks through him, jolting up his spine. He panted and moaned, Haridan's name twisted in each one. Then Haridan did something, rolled his hips and ground their bodies together hard, and Jamie was coming, breath rushing out of his lungs as he shot. Haridan arched and pumped into him harder and faster, then froze. With a deep growl Jamie felt in the pit of his stomach, Haridan came, filling him with heat.

"Holy..." Shaky, Jamie fell forward, not caring about the mess.

Haridan held him close, hands sliding up to cup his face. The kiss was soft and slow, the fire still there, though tempered for the moment. "Thank you," Haridan whispered on Jamie's lips.

"For what?" Jamie lifted his head to look at the vampire's face and for a moment, he thought maybe Haridan could see him, with whatever spell the man used.

"For coming to Rome with me."

# Chapter Twenty

Keeping himself completely shielded was an easy matter for Dio. He'd set up the meeting with Triarius well away from the halls of the Romanorum in a little, out of the way town south of London. The English pub was far different than an Italian café, but Dio appreciated both cultures. He sat unnoticed by the mortal patrons, having chosen this place for its lack of vampire clientele. When he felt Triarius' presence, Dio cast his shield outward to encompass his Son, making Triarius appear to be no more than an average-looking human being.

Triarius looked much the same as he once had, though he seemed to be a bit more cautious now. He sat down across from Dio and studied him for a moment before speaking. "This is not a social call, is it?"

"Unfortunately, no. I requested to meet you because of Aldrich. He's totally broken away from you, or I hope he has?" Dio paused, giving him a questioning look.

Triarius' jaw tightened and he looked away. "He has become... disillusioned. He finds me too old to lead, to unconcerned with conquering. I have not seen him in quite some time."

Dio rested his hand on the table, stopping just short of touching Triarius. "He kidnapped my grandson, Haridan, in an attempt to gain the Black Pearl Vision for himself. I'd already destroyed the damn necklace and made a fake that would devour whoever put it on. Luckily for Aldrich, one of his men thought to gain the power for himself."

"I am sorry, Father," Triarius said, staring down at the tabletop. "I knew long ago that he would be trouble. I never wanted to face the decisions that you've had to in the past—that of killing my own child. But if he is left free, he could destroy everything we've both worked for—you and the Romanorum, and myself and the Brotherhood." He looked up at Dio, pain evident in his pale eyes. "I swore to you I would never bring any harm to you. By that, I stand. You know I am a man of my word."

Dio knew exactly how damn hard the decision was, and there was nothing he could say or do that would make it easier. "I can destroy him, Triarius, but I prefer to give you the first choice in the decision because you are his Father."

Several seconds went by, in which Triarius studied the table, gaze drifting toward Dio's hand. "It was my mistake to create him," he said quietly. "It is my responsibility to see the deed done." His smile was rueful. "I often wondered what would have happened, had I not created the Brotherhood and left. Would I have gone down the road Aldrich is on now? Would you have destroyed me?"

"A decision I am thankful I never faced, Child. You know I don't interfere in the choices my Children make as long as both sides are left undisturbed. I understood your decision to be outside humanity even if I didn't agree with it. If I believed Aldrich could be reasoned with, I would insist on it, but his mind is unhinged with his own notions of power. He will take it at the cost of us all." Dio reached over, laying his hand on Triarius'. "There were a few times I didn't create wisely either; you are not alone."

After a moment, Triarius turned his hand, linking their fingers together. "Everything I am, I owe to you. I know I didn't understand that before, and there are still points on which I can't agree with you; but it will never change the fact that I am your Son."

With no more than a minor expenditure of energy, Dio shadowed them and kept the occurrence unobserved as they left the pub. Hidden in the darkness, Dio twined his fingers with Triarius' as they walked. "The past remains where it is. It is now that counts. Don't allow the past to disturb whatever peace we can find with each other. You may disagree with me with your last breath, but it will never change our relationship. It never has."

"Thank you." Triarius squeezed Dio's hand. "I will see that he is destroyed. I think, having had the time to reflect, that I now know what you meant about us existing alongside others. I still have my own viewpoints, some of which even Lance does not agree with, but I've become content to remain where I am, instead of pursuing matters best left alone."

"It just took time to come to that wisdom, Triarius. I am the public face of who we are supposed to be, and I have no problem being that. My affinity for mortals will never change. We are both best served by attending only to our concerns, and making sure the rest of the world remains ignorant of those not in the Romanorum. I am afraid you won't be able to convince Aldrich of that. You may try if you wish, but I would ask that you confine him until he sees reason."

"He will not listen to reason."

"Then I will leave it to you if you wish." Dio faced Triarius, his expression one of deep understanding. "I can remain with you for a time if you would like. It's been too long since last I saw you."

For the first time since their meeting, Triarius smiled. "I would like that."

* * *

Wakefulness arrived with the realization that it hadn't been a dream. Haridan smiled and tugged Jamie closer, kissing a bare shoulder. Jamie mumbled something, then scooted backward, lean body flush with Haridan's. After a moment, Jamie's right hand came back to rest on Haridan's hip.

"Good evening."

Jamie chuckled softly. "That'll take some getting used to." He shifted a little and Haridan groaned. "Feels good."

"What?" Haridan asked, amazed he got even that much out.

"Waking up beside you." The next movement couldn't possibly have been anything other than a blatant invitation, Jamie wiggling his ass just enough for Haridan's wakening cock to nestle in the warm crease.

"I would have to agree," Haridan whispered. Linking their fingers, he slid their joined hands around to the front, curling over Jamie's cock. Jamie moaned and thrust against their palms. "Want you."

"Got me." Jamie lifted his right leg and draped it over Haridan's hip, spreading himself open. "Please, Haridan."

Haridan released Jamie's hand and rolled over just enough to reach the lube on the bedside table. He slicked two fingers, then returned to where he'd been. Jamie lifted his leg a little higher and Haridan slipped his hand down, fingers skating over Jamie's entrance. "So hot," he murmured, easing inside.

Jamie gasped, nodded, body arching. "Yes...please..."

Haridan pumped his fingers slowly in and out, tongue licking Jamie's shoulder, then his neck, the temptation to bite almost as strong as the need to get inside the warm body pressed to his. He pushed deeper and Jamie cried out when his fingers stroked the smooth gland, that gorgeous body writhing beside him. Unable to wait any longer, Haridan replaced his fingers with his cock, sliding in deep.

"Oh, fuck," Jamie moaned. "Haridan."

Nodding, lips pressed to the thick vein in Jamie's neck, Haridan thrust, keeping his strokes slow and deep, grinding and rocking their bodies together. "Mine," he whispered. *Mine.*

Jamie shuddered and shouted when Haridan's fangs broke skin, the rush of blood sweetened as Jamie's body tightened around him, dragging Haridan over the edge. Panting, sated, Haridan licked the wounds and nuzzled Jamie's neck. Jamie's breathing evened out, but just when Haridan thought the young man was asleep, Jamie's whisper made him smile.

"Mine, too."

*Legends of the Romanorum, Book 5*
Necessary Evil

# Chapter Twenty-One

"A Son. You have a Son?"

"Vampirically speaking, yes."

Triarius didn't seem inclined to elaborate, which meant I had the rather unpleasant task of hounding him until he talked. Since he returned from his brief visit with Diocourides, Triarius had been quieter than usual. I had the feeling his Son, whom I'd heard nothing about before, had something to do with it. "You're angry."

"A bit," I admitted. "You having a Son doesn't bother me. It's the fact that you kept it from me."

Triarius sighed and stood. "What's done is done. You know now."

"Goddamn it!" I grabbed his arm before he could walk away, ignoring the look he gave me that would've scared the piss out of anyone else. "When were you planning on telling me?"

"And say what? Admit that I failed as a Father? That Aldrich was my worst mistake?" Triarius jerked free and backed me up against the wall, voice low. "Or would you rather I told you with his blood on my hands after I slit his throat?"

I swallowed. "You're going to kill him? Why?"

Triarius spun on his heel and started for the door. "Because he threatened to destroy everything my Father and I have worked for," he shot over his shoulder before slamming the bedroom door behind him.

What had just happened?

I blinked, still standing in the middle of the bedroom, wondering what I'd said to piss him off so much. A lot of parents, even vampires, I imagined, go through the whole 'I'm a bad parent' thing, right? So why was Triarius making such a big deal out of it? I sighed and raked a hand through my hair. There were times when I really didn't understand the man and his moods. He was over two thousand years old, sure, but he still acted like a damn teenager sometimes. Then again, having done the math, I'd finally realized a while back that he'd been eighteen when Dio turned him.

How I managed to get myself into these things, I didn't quite know.

One thing I did know, however, was that I needed to find him. I hated fighting with him, and I much preferred a smile or a breathy moan coming from those lips than a frown or an angry growl. Sighing, I left our bedroom and went in search of my temperamental lover. I found him in the Council room, staring out the window onto his underground empire. He didn't move or speak when I closed the door, but when I slipped my arms around his waist, one of his hands covered mine.

"I'm sorry."

"I know I am not perfect," he said quietly.

"No one has ever asked you to be. No one is perfect, Triarius."

"But as a ruler, as a Father, I'd hoped to be." He finally leaned back against me and I closed my eyes as I nuzzled his hair, breathing him in. "I'm tired, Lance."

"Somehow I don't think you mean in terms of needing sleep."

"No."

I knew this discussion would come eventually. "What do you want to do?"

Triarius sighed and laced our fingers together. "Retain control but give the Council of Elders rule beneath me. I want to spend our lives without worry about trivial matters I once concerned myself with."

In the past few months, I'd noticed the change in him. He seemed to have mellowed, and I wondered if maybe I'd been the cause of it. "Can I ask you something?"

"Of course."

"Do you regret anything? About us, me? Your views have changed so much in the past months, that I sometimes wonder if you wish-"

"Lance." Triarius turned and drew me close, hands threading through my hair to hold my head. "I regret nothing. I've only grown older, wiser, thanks in no doubt to my Father. And to Aldrich. I see myself in him, and I've come to realize that the roles have changed, from Dio and me, to me and Aldrich. Now I know where Dio was coming from when I always challenged him and his decisions. I can't sway Aldrich, though I wish I could. Our relationship has always been a volatile one, at war one moment, loving the next. Now, he only wishes my destruction, and the destruction of the Romanorum. That is something I cannot allow."

"Neither can I," I grumbled.

Triarius smiled and I reached up, tracing the lines on his face that he used to hide. Now, though, he didn't even flinch when I touched them. Maybe I was wrong about the teenager thing. Here before me was a grown man, one who'd lived through more than I could ever imagine. And I loved him more than anything else in this world.

"You don't have to be perfect," I said, fingertip following one particular scar down from his eye to just above his lips. "But you are for me. In everything you do, in the way you touch me, the way you watch me when you think I'm not looking, the way you let go when we're alone."

"You'll make a sentimental man out of me yet," he murmured. He kissed my fingers, then my palm, then my wrist, lips and tongue and fangs worrying my pulse point.

"And that's bad?" I asked breathlessly.

"No." He flicked my wrist with his tongue. "I treasure you," he whispered against my skin. "More than you know."

I swallowed, unable to find any words to express what his did to me. When he bit down, I gasped softly, shivering as his eyes drifted closed and his lips sealed around the wound, drinking deep. Though I was hard as stone, this wasn't about sex. It wasn't about physical sensations of any kind. I felt him deep within me, though, his essence pulsing through me, through my blood.

When he licked the wounds, I kissed him, arms sliding around his neck while his tightened around my waist. Pressed between the stone wall and his body, I forgot about everything else, and instead focused on the man in my arms, whose kiss could melt me where I stood.

He broke the kiss long enough to rid me of my shirt, then his lips drifted along my jaw. My head fell back as his kisses moved lower, teeth grazing my collarbone, my chest. Every touch made me burn, tiny trails of fire coaxed by his tongue on my skin. I threaded my fingers through his hair, shuddering when he caught one nipple and tugged it. Then came a sharp sting and I moaned as he sucked, entire body heating while he fed. His fingers skirted along the waistband of my jeans, popped the button, and eased the zipper down slowly. My cock pushed out, right into his waiting palm.

"Please," I whispered, thrusting gently as he stroked me. "Baby, please."

"Not here."

He didn't release me and shadows consumed us. When they faded, he backed me up to our bed, my jeans sliding down and off just before I settled. I watched him undress, each inch of skin revealed torturously slow. He knew I loved watching him and he indulged me whenever we slowed down enough. I sat up and held his hips, tracing his tattoo—the black spiraling sigil etched into his pale skin—with my tongue. Triarius moaned and cupped my head, his other hand slipping down to stroke his length. I took my time, worshipping every line, every curve, every swirl, until I finally reached his hand where it wrapped around the base of his cock.

Glancing up to his eyes, I moved his hand and flicked my tongue over the head, lapping at the beads of moisture glistening at the tip. Triarius growled softly, hand tightening in my hair. I closed my eyes and drew him in, dizzy from his taste.

"Lance..."

I smiled inwardly and swallowed him down to the root. Triarius hissed and both hands gripped my head, his hips beginning to move. I pulled back and off, almost chuckling at his groan. Then I slid back onto the bed and crooked a finger, beckoning him over. Triarius crawled over and kissed me, then turned. He straddled my head, then took me in hand, lips sealing over the head of my cock

"Oh, fuck." I almost forgot to reciprocate, but then he shifted and everything lined up perfectly. I spread him open and angled him down, licking his hole. Triarius moaned and the sound vibrated up my shaft so strong, I felt it in my throat. I thrust my tongue inside him and reached around and under him, fingers closing around him. I pumped him slowly while I licked and sucked his hole. His musk was addictive, something I'd never tire of. I held him tighter and pulled him until he let go of me and sat up.

"Lance. Fuck. Yes..."

There was nothing quite like reducing this man to babble. I plunged in and out, getting him ready. Before I was quite ready, though, he pulled away and spun around. He straddled me again and kissed me hard, taking my breath away as he sank down onto my cock in one smooth motion. Both of us groaned and I grabbed his waist, tugging him down until I was in to the hilt. Triarius grunted against my mouth, fangs nicking my bottom lip.

"Fuck me," he whispered.

"My pleasure."

He sat up, hands on my chest, and tipped his head back. I drew my legs up a little and anchored my feet, giving me some leverage as I began thrusting, lifting him and bringing him back down, driving deep. Triarius moaned and took himself in hand, eyes opening to look into mine as I ground us together between each stroke.

"Don't stop. Harder..."

I smiled and dug my fingers into his flesh, thrusting harder and faster. Triarius' strokes sped up, his eyes widening. Then on one particularly hard stroke, he shouted, entire body jerking. I grinned and hit his gland again and he bucked, come spraying up onto my chest as his ass tightened around me. That was all it took and I growled, grinding hard as I came. Triarius collapsed on top of me, panting and sweaty. I rubbed my hands up and down his back and kissed his neck.

"God, I love you," he murmured.

I chuckled. "Love you, too, baby. Even when you are a temperamental bastard."

"But I'm your temperamental bastard."

"Damn right."

# Chapter Twenty-Two

I awoke to find myself alone. It wasn't unusual for Triarius to be up before me, but a gut feeling told me this time was different. An undercurrent rippled through the air and had I still been mortal, I no doubt would've missed it. I got up and pulled on a pair of Triarius' lounge pants. Not bothering with a shirt, I left our room and sought out Triarius, using the link between us as a guide. I found him in the dining hall that nearly had the dubious honor of becoming my tomb at the hands of a scorned lover.

Triarius sat at one end of the long table, a decanter of something—blood-laced wine, most likely—passing back and forth between him and a man I'd never seen before. They talked as old friends might. *As old lovers.* I pushed that thought away immediately.

"Am I interrupting?"

Triarius smiled over at me and for a moment, I forgot we had company. Until he introduced us. "Lance," he said, extending a hand to me. I walked over and linked our fingers, letting him tug me onto his lap. "This is Apollonius, my general. He helped me create the Brotherhood and has been in America for a while."

I glanced at the man seated near us, fully intending to welcome him, and felt an instant jolt of attraction hit me like a punch to the gut. It had been the same way with Triarius—a lightning strike of lust that took my breath away. Realizing I'd not said a word, I offered Apollonius my hand. "Hi. Lance Shaw."

"My pleasure, Mr. Shaw. Or should I call you Lance?" His grip was strong and confident, his voice deep in timbre.

"Lance is fine," I said, nearly jumping out of my skin when Triarius' hand touched my upper thigh. I swallowed. A few inches higher and he'd feel the effect his general had on me. "So," I said, clearing my throat, "what brings you to Wales?"

Apollonius' gaze shifted and I felt Triarius nod behind me. "Business... and the desire to see an old friend."

*Old friend, my ass.*

It didn't take a rocket scientist to know how deep this particular friendship went. "Ah, gotcha." I extricated myself, discreetly but firmly, from Triarius' arms. "I'll be down in the bath if anyone needs me. Pleasure to meet you." I left before either man could say a word. I had to escape, as much from the thought of Triarius having someone else, as my disturbing attraction to that same person.

I had to force myself to not run down to the pool. I stripped off the pants and slipped into the warm water, shivering when the heat seeped into my body. Beyond the initial jealousy, I refused to examine the underlying truth of my reaction to meeting Triarius' general. Pushing those thoughts away, I tipped my head back and closed my eyes, willing the water to wash away the lingering, unwelcome desire. Strong arms suddenly enveloped me and I moaned when my lover's mouth descended on my neck, fangs scraping. I draped my own arms over Triarius' shoulders, legs going around his waist.

He didn't say anything, just thrust in deep, the burn making my entire body ache. I rode him there, trusting him to keep us above water as I slid up and down his cock. Triarius growled and spun us, slamming me against the edge. He kept me pinned as he took me without a word, fangs dragging along my throat. When he bit, I shouted, shaking in his arms as my body felt as if it was dissolving into the water. Triarius hissed and thrust hard, that gorgeous cock pulsing deep in my ass.

It took us a few minutes to finally regain our senses. I opened my eyes to find him watching me, his expression unreadable. He knew. Somehow, I had the feeling he knew. The knowledge in those eyes gave the post-orgasmic afterglow a rather bittersweet flavor. Triarius withdrew and pushed away from the wall, slipping under the water. I stayed where he left me, the knot in my stomach tightening.

"You love him," I said when Triarius resurfaced a few feet from me.

"Does that bother you?" Not a no, not a yes. But I took it as an affirmation of sorts. Triarius wasn't known for exuding affection.

I shrugged and turned my back to him, folding my arms on the side of the pool and resting my chin on them. I stared at three tiny rivers of water as they crept across the stone to merge into a small puddle, becoming one. "I don't know," I admitted.

I heard him moving through the water, but instead of getting out like I'd expected, he came up behind me and slid his arms around me, one at my waist and the other hand fanned out over my chest. "He has been by my side for a very long time."

"Longer than me." I refused to give into the heartache that threatened to tear me apart.

Triarius turned me, cupping my face and tilting it until I had no choice but to look him in the eyes. "Yes." When I tried to pull away, he kissed me. "But you are my soul, Lance."

* * *

"Who is he?"

Victoria continued checking the liquid in the vial, swirling it around, and didn't look up. "Apollonius? He's Triarius' most-trusted general."

"I thought Triarius didn't have anyone he trusts that much."

"They had a slight... falling out, when Triarius created Aldrich."

"Why?"

She sighed and set the vial in a holder on the table, then picked up another. "No matter what they say, I personally think it was an issue of jealousy. Apollonius didn't want to share Triarius with Aldrich."

That didn't bode well for me, but I kept that to myself. "So what can you tell me about Aldrich? Triarius said Aldrich was his worst mistake."

Victoria huffed. "I'll say. Aldrich is a spoiled brat, no different than he had been when Triarius met him. What Triarius saw in him, I still don't know. The subject is a touchy one, though."

"So I noticed," I muttered. "How is he going to kill Aldrich?"

Setting the second vial in another hole in the holder, Victoria glanced over at me, one eyebrow lifting. "He'll bleed him."

"Bleed him?" I swallowed. "As in...?"

She rolled her eyes and shook her head before putting the tray in a small refrigerator. "Depends on what sort of mood

Triarius is in. If he's resigned to the task, he'll be methodical about it and get my help. We'd strap Aldrich down, subdue him, and slit various veins to let the blood drain out slowly."

"Fuck. And if he's pissed?"

Victoria smirked. "He'll tear Aldrich open with his bare hands and teeth until nothing remains." At the look of horror I directed at her, she added, "Lance, you must understand: beneath these calm, somewhat civilized masks, we are monsters of nightmares. While we keep the beasts inside us at bay, there are times when those beasts must be unleashed."

"Remind me to never make him mad," I grumbled.

"Oh, make no mistake," Victoria said. "You harbor a beast just as dangerous and dark. You've only not learned to feel him."

I didn't say anything after that. Hell, I wasn't sure what to say. The beast thing? Okay, I could handle knowing it. It was the whole Triarius-Apollonius-Aldrich jealousy bit that left me wondering where I fit into the mess. I didn't doubt Triarius loved me, and I knew he loved Apollonius; but what if Apollonius was back to reclaim their relationship? What if I presented a challenge for him to brush aside? I shook my head, not really caring where I was going until I ran into someone.

"Sorry, I-" I stopped mid-sentence and stared up at the man of the hour. Or one of them, at least.

"My apologies," Apollonius said with a slight bow of his head. "I was on my way to the river to wait for a shipment. Would you care to join me?"

A thousand different answers warred in my mind, all essentially saying 'hell no'. With a table between us, with Triarius in the same room, I felt safe—from myself as much as the general. Without any buffers, however, the previous sensations rushed through me, making me dizzy with an attraction I was too terrified to acknowledge. Still, a walk to the river. We wouldn't be alone, at least. I nodded.

"Sure."

We started walking down to the river in silence. Around us, humans—ghouls, I knew now—and vampires bustled about their business. Only a few glanced our way, their expressions unreadable. Still new to the life and abilities of a vampire, I'd not learned how to read people's thoughts. The only one I could do with relative ease was Triarius, and I had the feeling that was primarily because we were lovers.

"You don't like me, do you?"

I shot a look up at Apollonius. "I..."

He smiled, the expression at once warm and yet disarming. "It's okay. You've no doubt heard about my history with Triarius. I imagine that would make any man jealous, when faced with a lover's former lover."

I cleared my throat, hoping I didn't sound as flustered as I felt. I shrugged in what I hoped was a nonchalant way. "It's no big deal. I mean, you're not here to steal him from me, and I do trust him."

"No, I am not here to steal him back." Apollonius stopped at the base of the stairs and motioned me to go before him down a dark path that led along the river's edge. "But it's not him you fear trusting, is it?"

"What?" I stopped and turned, only to find myself face to face with him. On instinct, my gaze slid down to his mouth, which curved into a sly smile, before I looked back up into his eyes. "What are you talking about?"

Apollonius stepped forward until there was no breathing room, whether we needed it or not. Heat radiated off of him, enveloping me, luring me. "Lance."

When I spoke, I cursed myself silently for the whispered, desperate sound. "Yes?"

"Stop fighting it."

"What?" I couldn't stop looking at his lips, wondering what they felt like on mine, or moving along my neck, or lower...

"Take what you want."

"But... he'll know." There it was, right between us, plain as day. I wanted him as badly as I wanted Triarius.

Apollonius closed the distance between us, lips barely brushing mine. "He already does," he whispered, then he kissed me.

Want and need rushed through me and I grabbed his head, tilting it to kiss him deeper. I crushed my mouth against his, sucked on his tongue. One of us bit down, though I didn't know who, and blood filled the kiss, sparking my hunger for more. I shoved him back against the rock wall and moved down, fangs sinking into his throat. Apollonius hissed and fisted a hand in my hair, but he didn't pull me away. Instead, he held me to him, legs spread so I stood between them, our bodies hard and pressing together. He tasted rich and thick, his blood holding a hint of Triarius, though not entirely. I didn't want to stop, ever, but I knew I couldn't take too much. I licked the wounds and he jerked my head back, kissing me just as hard as I'd kissed him.

# Chapter Twenty-Three

Commotion close to the keep broke the kiss abruptly and I stepped back, panting and staring at him. "I have to go." Without giving him a chance to say a word, I turned and ran back down the path toward the village, ignoring the protests my body and heart were making.

Several guards were heading up the steps and I fell in behind them, wondering what the trouble was. When I reached the top, Triarius was there. He didn't look my way, and I hoped he hadn't seen what transpired between me and Apollonius, though I thought we'd been out of sight. Apollonius said Triarius knew, but I didn't want to find out just how much.

"Aldrich was last seen in London. Prince Black knows he's there, and Diocourides has spoken with the prince. I want Aldrich brought to me, alive. Do I make myself clear?"

A chorus of 'yes, Lord's rang out and Triarius dismissed the men. When they were all gone, it left just the two of us there on the balcony. I went to him and ran my hands up and down his arms, his expression unreadable.

"You okay?"

"I'm preparing to kill my Son."

No, he wasn't okay. I drew him close and his hands fisted in the sides of my shirt. "Anything I can do?"

"You said you'd always stand by my side," he said quietly.

I nodded. "And I meant it."

"Then be there when the deed is done. Don't let me give into weakness when the time comes. He must be destroyed, Lance. He kidnapped my Nephew and threatened to kill Dio."

"I know." I swallowed, not entirely wanting to witness a vampire's death, but I'd made a promise. "And I'll be there."

"Thank you."

"You're welcome. How long do you think it'll take them to find him?"

Triarius sighed and gave me a slight hug before stepping away. He walked over to the rail and leaned on it. "I don't know. Aldrich isn't stupid. He knows I'm after him."

"I have a question for you."

"What?"

I took a deep breath and forged ahead. "I know from experience with you that there's a permanent connection, telepathically, between a Sire and the Son or Daughter. Can you sense where he is that way?"

Several seconds passed and I wondered if he was going to answer. His response didn't entirely surprise me.

"Yes," he said quietly. "But I've not used it. It can be done one-way, from Sire to Child, but..."

I knew where this was going without him finishing. "But the Father in you doesn't want to use it."

Triarius nodded.

I'd promised him I wouldn't let him back down, but how did a man convince his lover that a Child's destruction was necessary? I stood beside him, then after a moment, said, "Triarius, I vowed to you that I wouldn't let you fall prey to weakness."

"Help me, Lance."

I closed my eyes, the ache settling somewhere between my throat and stomach and all points in between. Those three words held a world of chaotic emotions that I'd never thought I'd feel or hear from the man beside me.

I'd learned enough of this world to know blood was the catalyst to everything. I needed Aldrich's blood.

"Let me feel him for you then. Give me some of his blood."

Triarius didn't answer with anything but a nod. He straightened back up and I followed him up into the keep. I had a feeling I knew where we were going and I was right as we started down the hall to Victoria's workroom. Triarius didn't knock and just opened the door. Another door on the far side opened as well and a disheveled-looking woman walked out, drawing her robe tight around her. She wasn't Victoria, nor was she Marie. I looked at Triarius as the woman smiled demurely and hurried out the door we'd come in through.

"One of Victoria's lovers," he said. "She doesn't have a sexual relationship with Marie."

Ah, that explained it. I hadn't realized Victoria had any lovers. Victoria came out a moment later, dressed in tight pants and a plain white button-down shirt. I had to admit, she was a beautiful woman. She eyed us both warily.

"Something tells me you're going to make me work tonight."

Triarius chuckled a little. "Not really. I need... I need a vial of Aldrich's blood."

One eyebrow lifting, Victoria glanced from Triarius to me, then back to him. "I see. Well, that I can do easily." She went to the line of coolers in the back and opened one of them. After a few minutes of muttering, she closed the top and came back to us, carrying a thin vile of chilled blood. Instead of handing it to Triarius, though, she handed it to me.

"How did you know?"

"Because I know him." Her smile, directed at Triarius, was affectionate. "Speaking as a Mother, I can tell you that you have your work cut out for you, Lance."

"Thanks, I think." I took the vial and looked over at Triarius. "Ready?"

"No. But I have no choice." He kissed Victoria on the cheek, which surprised me since I'd never seen him do anything of the sort before, and then we left. "I want to do this in our chambers, away from others."

"Understandable. Anything I should know?"

"Keep it one-way. Don't let him know you're reaching out to him. He wouldn't know you anyway, but I don't trust him and if he has a connection to you, he could cause trouble."

"Like...?"

Triarius stopped at our door and opened it. "Like attacking my primary weakness."

Oh. I blinked. Jesus, what was I getting myself into doing this?

We went into our room and he closed the door, locking it. I went to the bed and sat down, scrubbing my hands over my face. "Okay. Follow the thread in his blood to him, but close myself off. Right?"

Triarius gave me the vial. "Yes."

"Will you feel me if I close myself off like that?"

"Depends on how strong your defenses are, and how strong I am." When I looked up at him warily, he smiled. "Don't worry."

"I trust you," I sighed.

I pulled out the stopper, took a deep breath, and tipped the vial. Slightly cool blood poured over my tongue and I closed my eyes. I sensed Triarius in it, but not as strong as I'd expected. Then I felt something unfamiliar, a tug on my awareness, a different twist in the taste itself. I knew it was Aldrich and I felt Triarius lay me down. I focused inward, shielding myself as Triarius had taught me, and followed the thread through the blood. I imagined everyone envisioned it differently, but for me, it was a silver-white string, like what I'd always heard astral cords as being. It grew stronger the longer and farther I followed it, and then full awareness slammed into me.

*I was in a warehouse, somewhere, London, I think. There were other vampires and ghouls, but no pure humans. Or so I thought. A young woman screamed as men dragged her in through a doorway. I felt Aldrich smile, felt him rise. He approached the woman and circled her where she lay crumpled on the dirty floor. When he kicked her ribs, I flinched, wanting to cry out for her. He fisted a hand in her hair and jerked her head back. Fear radiated in overwhelming waves from her bloodshot, tear-filled blue eyes.*

*"Such a pretty thing," Aldrich purred. "Tell me, do you taste as sweet?"*

*"Please don't hurt me! I promise I won't tell anyone..."*

*"Oh, sweets, you won't live long enough to walk out of here. I have no worry about your loose tongue."*

*He drew a knife slowly across her throat and bent to lap the blood. I tasted the coppery thickness in my own mouth, and it made me sick. Aldrich threw her to the floor and several vampires descended on her, her last screams muffled as they all fed. Aldrich turned to someone else.*

*"My Father thinks I am afraid to face him." Aldrich slid the blade across his tongue and shivered. "So it's time to pay the old man a visit, I think. We leave in two hours for Wales."*

*"Yes, my Lord."*

I snapped back into myself and gasped. I felt someone near me, but I shoved them away and rolled off the bed, landing hard on my hands and knees as I threw up the last blood I'd had. Shivering and sweating, I fell backward into strong arms. Something cool touched my forehead.

"He's coming," I whispered, voice raspy. "He's coming here."

# Chapter Twenty-Four

I hadn't realized I'd fallen asleep until I woke up to voices around me. I blinked my eyes slowly, forcing away the echoes of the screams I'd heard during my little spying adventure. I was in our bedroom, and when I turned my head, I saw Triarius and Apollonius talking, both standing over the table across the room. They were bent over a sheet of paper, voices low. I licked my dry lips and shuddered. If I'd known projecting would have such a strong aftereffect, I probably wouldn't have been dumb enough to do it.

"You're awake."

Though I didn't remember closing my eyes, I opened them again to find Triarius sitting on the bed beside me. "I think so."

"How do you feel?"

"Like I've been hit by a damn truck."

He nodded. "That tends to happen sometimes. It's a result of being snapped back into your body while projecting. Ideally, you'd come back slowly."

"I'll take your word for it." I looked around and realized Apollonius had left. "Where did he go?"

"Who? Apollonius? I've put him in charge of bolstering defenses down here. Since your pronouncement, things have gone into an uproar."

"Can Aldrich get down here?"

Triarius sighed and stood. "There are several ways to get into this place, all of which are guarded. However, like me, Aldrich has control over the shadows and, having been here before, he can get back that way."

I sat up a bit, propped on my elbows. "So you're going to need a personal guard then."

"And you." He glanced over at me. "You're just as likely a target as I am, Lance."

"But I didn't create the Brotherhood. I'm nowhere near as powerful as you. Killing me would-"

"It would be a direct attack on me," Triarius interrupted. He came back and sat down. "Don't you see? As my lover, and my co-ruler, you are the perfect target."

I studied him in silence for a moment. "Then what do we do?"

"We organize our personal guards."

I didn't bother to ask if Apollonius would be part of Triarius' guard. That was a given. "Okay, so let's do it then."

"First things first. You need to feed. You lost a lot of blood."

"No shit."

"How do you want it? Donor or a bottle?"

I grabbed him and tugged him down onto his back, then leaned over him. "You."

Without giving him a chance to respond, I bent and sank my fangs into his throat. Triarius growled and fisted a hand in my hair, pressing me tighter to his neck. His blood, rich and thick and laced with unbelievable power, flowed over my tongue, sating my hunger quicker and better than any donor ever could. When I felt him shudder beneath me, I bit harder. Triarius cried out and shook, the blood turning addictively sweet as he came. I smiled and licked the wounds closed.

"Fuck," he whispered. "Remind me to feed you more often."

The door opened just as I had my hand poised to undo Triarius' pants. We both snarled at the intrusion until we realized it was Victoria. She didn't look particularly amused.

"If you two aren't too busy, I have something for you to look at."

I sighed and crawled off of Triarius, who stood and grimaced. Chuckling, I waved Victoria out. "We'll be there in a second." She rolled her eyes and shut the door. I grinned as Triarius peeled his pants off. "Note to self: undress you before I feed."

"Agreed." He cleaned up and put on another pair of pants before we headed to Victoria's workroom.

She urged us in, looked around the hallway, then closed and locked the door. "You're gonna love this." She hurried over to one of her work tables and set up slides on two microscopes. "Here. Look."

Triarius and I exchanged glances, then we each peered through a microscope. Then we switched.

"They're identical," I said, not quite understanding what the hell I was looking at to begin with.

"Exactly." Victoria crossed her arms, looking rather proud of herself, though why, I had no idea.

"So... what is it?"

"Formula," Triarius said quietly. He moved between the scopes a couple of times, then looked from me to her. "She's duplicated it."

"What? I thought the Brotherhood didn't create new vampires."

"We don't," Victoria said.

Okay. Now I really was confused. "I don't get it. Why the need to make the formulas then?"

Victoria pulled a sheet of paper from a folder and handed it to me. Names I recognized jumped out as I skimmed it and I started reading it fully. While I didn't read slow enough to gather any major details, I did realize that I held a piece of history in the making in my hands. According to the letter, Victoria and Triarius now worked with the Romanorum in coming up with stronger formulas.

"Holy shit." I looked up at her, then at Triarius. "You're working *with* the Romanorum now?"

"I am."

I read over the paper again, noting such names as Cornelius, who was Prince Mael Black's court mage, Mael Black himself, Diocourides, and several others in the Romanorum. "Does this mean... you're coming out of hiding?" I asked cautiously.

"There are still those in the Romanorum who would just as soon see me dead," Triarius said. "But in time, yes, that is precisely what it means."

"What do the others in the Brotherhood think?"

"The Elders are firmly behind the decision. Those who disagree will not be allowed to survive. Most of them have already joined my Son."

"This is why Aldrich kidnapped Dio's Grandson, isn't it? But how did he know?"

Victoria put the slides away in a box and offered an answer. "I'm assuming that one of those who disagreed with Triarius' choice found out about this development, the details of it, and defected to Aldrich with the information."

"That's possible," Triarius said. "No matter how it became known, Aldrich knows and he realized I wasn't going to pursue any action against the Romanorum, that I was, in fact, working with them to develop more and stronger formulae, and he took matters into his own hands. That decision, of course, will cost him his life, and the lives of those who follow him."

"Babe," I said, handing the paper back to Victoria, my attention on Triarius, "you have the most dysfunctional family of the fucking century."

Triarius smirked. "To put it mildly."

We left Victoria to tinker with her new formula and headed for the throne room.

"You aren't a rogue, are you?" I'd always thought of him as one, since a rogue was a vampire who did or had killed mortals.

"Yes. When Dio created the first formula, we all drank it."

"So what happens if you leave the safety of this place and someone who doesn't know you aren't like that anymore decides to kill you?"

"Then that person would be put to death as well," he said. "The Romanorum as a whole knows I haven't killed a mortal in a very long time. I've not had a need to, even before you came along. Most of the threats were just that: scare tactics to ensure obedience."

"So you wouldn't have killed me."

He grinned at me before opening the door to the throne room. "Never was my intention."

Many others were already gathered around the room, the Elders along one wall. I followed Triarius up to the dais where our chairs stood and we sat down, the room eerily silent. Most of the people kept their gazes focused solely on Triarius.

"I assume you all wonder why I have called this court since it is not something I deign to do very often," he said. There were a few nods, a few looks exchanged. "Make no mistake: what I am about to announce has the full support of the Elders. Should anyone disagree with the decision, know you will not make it out of this keep alive."

I swallowed. When Triarius made that threat, he kept to it. I'd seen him kill before, when a spurned ghoul had seen fit to attempt to take me out of the picture by entombing me in one of the dining halls. The result had been terrifying, his death showing me just how ruthless my lover could be. As I scanned the others in the room, I saw expressions ranging from positive interest to outright fear.

"I created this Brotherhood because I disagreed with Diocourides and the Romanorum. I felt humans were beneath us, while my Father did not feel the same. That was a long time ago. I am older now, wiser. I must admit to owing a lot of my change of heart to my companion Lance Shaw." I shot a disbelieving look at him, but he continued. "Since our first meeting, I've come to realize that not all humans are to be blamed for the evil, only a practiced few. To that extent... I have made an arrangement with the Romanorum that will change the Brotherhood forever.

Whispers filled the room and one of the vampires, not an Elder, stepped up. "My Lord, what happens to those of us who have killed? Some of us took the formula, and thus are branded forever as rogues. What protects us from death should we venture out of the safety of this place?"

"Diocourides has pardoned us," Triarius said, earning himself a chorus of gasps. "All of us. And should anyone attempt to harm any one of us, he or she would be put to death."

"So we have allied with the Romanorum?" the vampire asked. At Triarius' nod, the vampire smiled slowly. "I can go home..."

"We all can, my friend," Triarius said. "I will maintain the keep here, but as of this meeting, you are all free to leave and know you are safe within the halls of the Romanorum once more."

The cheers that filled the room were deafening. I just sat there, stunned beyond belief. The Inferi Brotherhood had, for all intents and purposes, dissolved right before my eyes. A huge piece of Romanorum history just played out before me and I still hadn't processed the fact that I could leave without fear of death.

Triarius squeezed my hand and in a daze, I looked over at him. "Have you ever been to Rome?"

# Chapter Twenty-Five

After the court meeting, I went back to our room. My God. I still couldn't believe Triarius was disbanding the Brotherhood. I thought maybe I was just as shocked as his court when he made the announcement. He hadn't said a word to me, which irritated me a bit. I grabbed a pair of clean pants and figured I'd ask him when I saw him why he hadn't told me. Pants in hand and the thought of a nice, relaxing bath in mind, I left in search of my ever-surprising lover.

I found Triarius and his general in the bath, Apollonius swimming through the water like the man had been born to it. Triarius sat on the side, leaning back on his palms, feet in the water. They talked each time Apollonius came up and I stood for a moment and watched them. It was easy to see the respect and... love... that they held for each other. They acted as best friends around others, but in private, the truth became clear. Since my kiss with Apollonius by the river, I'd tried to avoid the man, terrified of something more happening. As Apollonius swam up to Triarius, I discovered something even more worrying: I wanted to see them together.

Apollonius said something, though I couldn't hear what. Triarius reached out and touched his general's face, fingers slipping down to trace those sinful lips. I swallowed hard.

"And what would you have of me, my lord, if you could?"

"All of you," Triarius said. "I hope that Lance comes around and sees how good we could be together."

Brow furrowing, I stared at Triarius, not quite believing what I'd just heard.

"I kissed him."

"Mm, did you? And did you taste him?"

Apollonius shuddered, eyes sliding closed as Triarius' hand drifted along his neck. "He tasted me."

I shivered as well. I knew that touch like no other, knew what magic those fingers could produce. Triarius descended into the water and my private fantasy played out before my eyes as my lover's mouth met his general's. My cock pressed against my pants and I couldn't stop myself from touching. I traced my length as Triarius plundered Apollonius' mouth, the moans creating an erotic soundtrack for me. When the kiss ended, Triarius gripped Apollonius' hair and tugged the man's head back. A low growl followed and the sweet scent of blood, tinged with arousal, drifted right through me.

"Please..." Apollonius whispered. "I am yours."

Triarius pulled back and licked his lips. "Show me."

Apollonius got out of the water and spread out on a towel. Triarius followed and stood before him, water running in rivulets off his decorated body. I licked my lips, wanting desperately to touch, to taste. Triarius went to his knees and parted Apollonius' thighs. The general's cock was thick, the hair around the base dark. Precome glistened at the tip and Triarius scooped it up with his fingertip. He sucked the liquid from his skin and my cock twitched in time with Apollonius' moan.

"Master..."

"Shh, here, I am no master," Triarius whispered. Braced over Apollonius' body, he leaned down and kissed him, their cocks pressing together. I wanted so much to join them, to kiss Apollonius the moment Triarius pushed inside him. It happened so fast, I almost missed it. One moment Triarius was kissing him, the next, the general shouted, back arching as Triarius' cock plunged inside him.

"Triarius!"

Before I realized it, I had stepped out from my hiding place. Neither of them stopped, but Apollonius watched me approach. I knelt down and he reached up, fingers fisting in my hair as he tugged me down for a hard kiss. I moaned and Apollonius grunted. When I broke the kiss, I looked up to find Triarius watching us both, lust darkening his eyes.

"Touch him."

I thought Triarius meant for me to touch Apollonius, but hands immediately began working my pants open. When the general pulled my cock out, I gasped and thrust into his fist. He urged me closer and I nearly fell over him when his lips closed around the crown.

"Fuck!" I grabbed his head and let myself go, fucking his mouth with quick, shallow strokes. "Gonna come," I panted.

"Yes," Triarius hissed. He slammed into Apollonius twice and let out a deep growl, hips jerking.

Apollonius' eyes rolled back and he sucked harder, moaning around my shaft and he and I came at the same time, his spunk hitting my thigh as mine shot down his throat. I pulled out and collapsed back onto my ass on the stone floor, beyond dazed. Triarius leaned down and kissed his general, humming no doubt at the taste of me on Apollonius' tongue.

"What..." I couldn't catch my breath long enough to finish.

Triarius chuckled and eased out. He crawled over to me and kissed me slowly, softly. "Do you desire him?"

"I..." I stared up into my lover's eyes, knowing damn well I couldn't lie. "Yes."

"Good. I want you both in my bed."

"Now?"

He smiled. "Always."

"You're a greedy bastard," I shot back, smiling to soften the words.

"I am." Triarius bore me down, the stone cool through my shirt. "But I am *your* greedy bastard."

"And his..."

He paused and studied me for a moment. "And his. Does that bother you?"

I thought about it and realized it really didn't. "At first, I think it did. I hadn't thought of the possibility of all three of us. And I didn't *want* to want him."

"Ah, but you did," Triarius said, fingertip tracing my lips. "You do."

I nodded and licked his finger. "I do. Can I ask you a question?"

"Anything."

"Has he ever fucked you?"

One eyebrow rose and Triarius remained silent for a few seconds. Then he shook his head. "No. When we were lovers before, it was... a different situation."

"You were afraid of letting him, worried it would make you seem weak," I finished for him.

"Yes."

"And now?"

Triarius glanced over to the pool where Apollonius had resumed swimming. "Now..."

An image took hold in my head and refused to let go. I rolled us, putting Triarius beneath me, and I nuzzled his neck, nipping and licking the flesh. He moaned and threaded his fingers through my hair.

"I want to see him," I whispered, letting my fangs scrape just enough to make Triarius shudder, "with his cock buried deep in your ass."

"Lance." Triarius gasped and I felt his cock flex between us. Oh, somebody liked that idea.

"And then... I want you both..." I moved my mouth back up to his ear. "Inside me."

Triarius hissed and dug his fingernails sharply into my biceps. "And you will get your wish, of that I am certain."

# Chapter Twenty-Six

"Master, he's here," a guard said from the doorway.

I snapped my head up just as Triarius slipped out from beneath me. "Already?"

"Apollonius, assemble the others," Triarius ordered as he dressed. "Lance, come with me."

I had no idea what to expect, but I didn't have a chance to ask as he grabbed my waist and the shadows engulfed us. When they faded, we were standing in the throne room. Triarius sat in his throne, and I did the same just as the door burst open.

"Unhand me!" A young man jerked free of the two guards who had him, then turned a dark glare on us.

"Where is my Son?" Triarius asked, voice deceptively quiet. Shadows began creeping from the corners of the room, reminding me of the last time I'd seen Triarius pissed.

"He sent me with a message," the vampire before us sneered. "Renounce the Romanorum, or abdicate your throne."

Triarius let out a short, sharp laugh. "And do what? Turn it over to him? He is useless, pathetic."

Only then did the vampire seem to notice the shadows. He took two steps backward, his fear growing palpable. "He is powerful," he argued, eyes darting from Triarius to the shadows and back. "More than you realize."

Triarius rose from his throne slowly, like a slumbering cat just awakening. "He is weak," he said as he stalked the vampire across the room. The vampire backed up further until he hit the throne room door. "And make no mistake..." Triarius lifted his right hand and a mass of black shadows swirled and hovered over his palm. "Aldrich and everyone who follows him will die."

Triarius blocked my view, but when the shriek came, I instinctively squeezed my eyes shut. Fear bolted through me a split second before the explosion. I dove off the throne for Triarius seconds before the door shattered. A group of vampires, ones I'd never seen before, strode in through the cloud of dust and debris. Triarius stood slowly and dabbed at the blood on his lip as the cut healed.

"Well, well, if it isn't the mighty Triarius."

The group parted and a man stepped to the middle of the room. I didn't have to ask to know who he was. Aldrich radiated arrogance, more so than his Father ever had. Aldrich spared a dismissive look at me as I stood as well.

"A new toy?" He sniffed the air, then his lips curled back into a ruthless, deadly grin. "A new Child? And I thought I was the only one..."

"Where are my men?"

"Oh... you mean our dear friend Apollonius?"

We both followed Aldrich's gaze toward the door. Several more vampires entered, dragging a battered man with them. My jaw dropped when I saw who it was.

"What have you done?" Triarius snarled, advancing on Aldrich. He stopped abruptly when four vampires lifted crossbows armed with sharpened stakes at him.

"I really had hoped we could discuss this like civilized men," Aldrich sighed.

The men holding Apollonius dropped him unceremoniously on the floor, but I didn't dare move. Not when my other lover was held at stake-point. Apollonius didn't move, but when one of the guards shoved him onto his back, I realized why. A gaping hole was all that remained of his heart. That knowledge hit me a like a blow to the gut, to know that this strong man had been taken down.

Then Aldrich held up his hand, the general's heart beating faintly in it. Blood dripped to the stone floor and the scent permeated the air. "He never saw it coming. He always was too dependent on brawn. Then again, I've grown stronger since he last saw me..."

A commotion rose outside the room and I saw my chance. I rushed the group of men holding the crossbows, taking two of them down hard, their skulls splitting with the impact on stone. I snarled and whirled on another one, my fangs and claws lengthening as I lunged for him, shredding his face and neck. He screamed and I felt a sharp bolt of pain in my side, but it didn't stop me as I tore him apart, blood spraying onto me and the wall. I left him and growled at the last one as I stalked him into a corner. He wasn't a vampire. He was a ghoul. A fucking ghoul.

His crossbow hit the floor the second I jumped him. I dug my claws into his skin and split him open, my fangs tearing bites out of his throat. Bloodlust ruled me, anger and pure hatred fueling the beast. I gulped down mouthfuls of blood, not stopping even when he ceased to struggle. When hands took hold of me, I spun, ready to kill again.

"Lance!" A sharp slap connected with my face and my vision cleared. Victoria stared at me, her expression unreadable.

I looked around, only to find that the rest of Triarius' guards had subdued Aldrich's. Apollonius was nowhere in sight. "Where...?"

"Marie has the general. She's a healer."

"And Triarius?" He wasn't in the room either. Neither was Aldrich.

Victoria smiled slowly. "Undoing a mistake. He's in the dungeon."

Despite the stickiness of blood and gore all over my clothes and skin, I hurried down the hall, then deeper into the keep, into the bowels of the mountain. I heard the screams long before I found them, the sight still a shock even after what I'd done.

Silver chains kept Aldrich's arms taut above his head, the joints no doubt stretched to their limits. The skin of his wrists sizzled and smoked and he shrieked as Triarius circled him.

"I should never have created you," he hissed. "You're an abomination, a fucking disease to be rid of."

"Father, please!"

Triarius' pain struck me hard and fast and nearly had me doubled over. It flowed in nauseating waves through me, so strong that I barely heard his silent plea for help. Steeling myself against the onslaught, I entered the room. Aldrich shook, his bare skin striped with fresh and dried blood. Triarius stopped behind him and Aldrich closed his eyes, muttering something under his breath. I caught Triarius' gaze over Aldrich's shoulder. My presence was all he seemed to need. With a handful of hair, Triarius jerked his Son's head back and ripped into his throat. I shuddered and watched Aldrich's eyes widened, his last screams echoing through the dungeon.

Triarius tore away abruptly, blood flowing down his chin. "It is done."

With that, he was gone, consumed in shadows.

# Chapter Twenty-Seven

I left the dungeon, forcing back the hunger that the scent of fresh blood welled up, and went in search of Apollonius. I had the distinct feeling it would take both of us to bring Triarius back from the darkness I now felt within me. His moods reflected in my mind, and this one was dark and dangerous, far exceeding mere brooding. He'd just destroyed his Son, I couldn't quite blame him.

I went to Victoria's workroom and found the door to her private chambers open. Marie and Victoria were both in there, and Apollonius lay on the bed between them. The hole in his chest was gone and Marie was washing the blood from him as Victoria supported his head so he could drink from a bottle. When Victoria saw me, she smiled.

"Hey." I sat on the end of the bed and waited until Marie and Victoria left quietly before continuing. "You look like hell."

Apollonius cracked a slight smile. "I feel like it. Where is he?"

I stared down at my hands in my lap. "I don't know. He killed Aldrich, then he just disappeared. I can't feel anything but a void."

"Hey..." Apollonius touched my arm, fingers stroking gently. "He's not lost. Trust me. He's strong enough, even for this."

"I didn't think he was going to do it. I felt him falter, so I went in, just to be there."

Apollonius nodded. "Killing a Child is never a pleasant task, but as you've seen, there are times when it is necessary."

I shuddered and with only the slightest tug from him, lay down beside Apollonius. Then I shot back up. "I'm filthy."

He chuckled and jerked me back down, ignoring my feeble protests. "Relax, Lance."

For someone who'd literally had his heart ripped out, he was quite strong. He held me down without much effort, though in truth, I didn't want to move. He lowered his head and kissed me, just a slight pressure, a brush of his lips. I groaned and grabbed his head, thrusting my tongue into his mouth. Apollonius growled softly and pinned my arms to the pillow above my head, his fangs scraping my bottom lip as he pulled back a little.

"Shall we go find our brooding lover?" he asked.

"You sure you're up for moving?"

"Absolutely." He got up and held out a hand to me. I just shook my head and took his hand as I stood. "What?"

"You never were a good patient, were you?"

He smirked at me over his shoulder as he led the way out. "No." I barely caught Victoria's disapproving but defeated scowl before Apollonius tugged me out the door.

"Have you turned anyone?" I asked as we walked down the hall.

Apollonius shook his head. "No. It just never appealed to me. And after seeing what happened with Aldrich, and again with his Son, it just made me more certain that I didn't want to do it."

"Wait." I stopped, brow furrowing. "Aldrich has a Son?"

"Oh, yes. Aldrich created him to infect London with rogues."

My jaw dropped. "The ones Mael Black and his companion destroyed?"

"The very ones. Though Aldrich's Son is safe and sound and not a rogue."

"Okay... So who is he?"

Apollonius grinned over at me as we resumed walking. "Companion to Prince Black's court mage."

"Holy shit. He's..."

"Yes, Brandon Davies is Triarius' Grandson."

I blinked. "Does Brandon know this?"

"I don't think so. He didn't know who Aldrich was when Aldrich turned him and set him loose to kill. Cian Carmichael found him before he could kill anyone, though. And well, you know how the rest of that goes if you've kept track of vamps above ground."

"Yeah, I do. I've met Prince Black briefly, and I've seen Cornelius and Brandon, but never spoken to either one. I take it Triarius knows about Brandon?"

"He does, and he's grateful to Carmichael for finding Brandon before things got out of control."

We went down to the bath, but found it empty. That's when I realized exactly where Triarius had gone. I tugged Apollonius back up the steps, then up another set toward the small Council room. I opened the door and saw him leaning against the wall, staring out his favorite window to the world he'd built below. I let go of Apollonius and went to Triarius, slipping my arms around him. After a few seconds, one of his hands came up to rest over mine. Apollonius joined us, blocking Triarius' view by standing halfway in front of him.

"You are a persistent son of a bitch," Triarius muttered to his general. He must've smiled, because Apollonius did as well.

"Did you think we would let you carry this on your own?" Apollonius asked him.

I turned my hand over, linking my fingers with Triarius'. I kissed his neck and whispered, "You should know better by now."

"Yes, I should." Triarius reached up with his other hand and cupped Apollonius' face. "Are you all right?"

"Better than ever." Apollonius drew Triarius' hand down and stepped closer. I felt Triarius' moan vibrate his throat and looked up to find them kissing. The sight of the general's lips and tongue sliding over Triarius' made my knees weak.

"We need a bed," I groaned. "Especially if you two keep that up."

One of them chuckled and their kiss ended. Before I could say another word, Apollonius' mouth came down on mine, scrambling my thoughts into an indefinable jumble. A hand, whose I didn't know, stroked my hip, then down between me and Triarius to cup me through my pants.

"Okay," I panted, stepping back. "Bed. Now."

Arm around Triarius' waist, Apollonius grabbed me and hauled me close before shadows shifted us to our room. Only then did Triarius step away and undress. For a moment, Apollonius and I both just stood there, drinking the man in with hungry gazes. Triarius sat on the bed and scooted back, thighs spread, cock hard and painting a slick trail over his stomach.

"Well? Are you two going to stand there all night and stare? Or are you going to join me?"

That broke us out of our stupor and we both stripped, clothing landing wherever. Then we each took a side, crawling across the bed to close in on him. I thought back to them in the bath and groaned. I leaned over and licked Apollonius' lips.

"I want to watch you fuck Triarius."

Apollonius glanced down at Triarius, who lay sprawled on the bed, one hand idly stroking his cock. No words were spoken as Triarius shifted, legs spreading to bracket Apollonius. I grabbed the oil and licked Apollonius' jaw as I slicked his cock, fist sliding up and down slowly.

"Fuck," he whispered, a shiver betraying the stalwart control he tended to have. "Enough." He seized my hand and angled it downward. "Get him ready?"

"No." I coated Apollonius' fingers with the oil. "You do it."

He smiled and leaned down, one hand bracing him over Triarius. "Are you sure?" he asked our lover.

"Please..." The word was barely audible, but the need in Triarius' eyes made it perfectly clear. He drew his legs up and when Apollonius' fingers breeched his body, Triarius gasped, eyes rolling back as his hips rocked. "Yes..."

Apollonius groaned and pushed in a third finger. I felt Triarius shudder while I lay beside him and I kissed his neck, fangs scraping gently. He moaned and turned his head, giving me room to play. Out of the corner of my eye, I saw Apollonius withdraw his fingers and then he lined himself up. With a slowness that made even me ache, he pushed into Triarius. I whimpered and bit, unable to stop. Triarius cried out and Apollonius took the opportunity to thrust in hard and deep. Triarius fisted a hand in my hair, pinning me to his neck, and I swallowed mouthfuls of blood as he bucked, riding his general's cock the way he'd ridden mine plenty of times.

It was over before I knew it. Triarius jerked, chanting unintelligible words under his breath as his sweetened blood flowed over my tongue. Apollonius growled and then they were kissing, the general slamming into Triarius as he came. The scents, of semen, of blood, filled the air and I was lost, crying out against Triarius' throat as my own cock throbbed, pulsing heat against his side.

Breathless, I collapsed against him, half on, half off, barely managing to lick the wounds on his neck closed. A few moments later, I felt a kiss on my shoulder and Apollonius moved to the other side. With my arm draped over Triarius, my fingers brushing Apollonius' hip, I slipped into a much-needed, restful sleep.

* * *

When I awoke, I realized just how much I *hurt*. While vampires healed quickly, the residual aches still lingered. I tried not to think about what all had happened the night before, especially in the throne room. Screams still echoed in mind, but I endured them. I'd never thought myself capable of killing anyone, but the thought—the sight—of my lovers in pain had been what spurred me into action. Now I knew what Victoria meant by the beast inside me. I shuddered at the memory, thankful that not all the details remained. I wasn't sure I really wanted to know what all I'd done to those men.

I sat up slowly and waited for my equilibrium to return. In twenty-four hours, I'd seen death, fucked two amazing men, and torn grown men to pieces with my bare hands and teeth. It was enough to make me want to lie down and sleep again. Instead, I got out of bed, wondering where my lovers were. I slipped on a pair of thin pants and left the room.

I found them both in the small, makeshift village, helping several others load things onto one of the river barges. Triarius and Apollonius both looked up at the same time and smiled. I'd never tire of seeing those expressions. I grabbed a box and began helping them, and soon we were done. Triarius issued orders to have another barge sent back down and then he joined me and Apollonius where we stood near one of the houses.

"Are you going to miss it?" I asked him, slipping my arms around him to draw him in close. Apollonius leaned against us both, chin resting on my shoulder.

"A little," Triarius sighed. "Not everyone is leaving. Some have grown so accustomed to living here that they don't wish to reenter the outside world. I've given Victoria and Marie control of the keep."

"They're not going?"

"No. Victoria is quite content where she is, and Marie isn't old enough to leave her side yet. They'll keep this place open for those who wish to remain."

"What about us?" Apollonius asked quietly.

Triarius studied us both. "I want to see my Grandson. He deserves to know about his Father. Then... I want to return home—back to Rome."

"How do you think Brandon will handle things?" I asked.

Triarius shrugged. "I have no idea. But I do know that Black's court mage has become Brandon's adoptive Father and his companion, so at least Brandon is safe."

I smiled and stroked my fingers down Triarius' cheek. "You know, you have more of a heart than you think you do."

"I'm only a monster when I need to be," Triarius answered. "When it's necessary."

"You're no monster. Just a very driven man."

Triarius smiled and pressed closer. Apollonius shifted until he stood behind me, effectively pinning me between them. "I don't know what we'll face in Rome."

"When are we leaving?" I asked him.

"Soon." He glanced up at Apollonius. "Though for now, I want you both alone. When we reach Rome, I have no idea when we'll get the time to ourselves, at least not for a while."

My eyes slipped closed when I felt the general's lips brush my neck. "I want you both," I whispered, "at the same time."

One of them growled, though I couldn't tell who, and Triarius kissed me hard. Shadows consumed us and the next thing I knew, they were stripping my clothes off, kisses and licks and bites landing on every bare patch of skin they revealed. I shuddered and spread my legs when Apollonius knelt behind me, and bracing myself on Triarius' shoulders as he went to his knees in front, I cried out. The moment Triarius swallowed my cock, Apollonius spread me open and thrust his tongue into my ass. I panted and shook, the dual sensations driving me absolutely mad.

Then they both stood and steered me backward toward the bed. Triarius undressed and lay down, his fist pumping his hard cock as I straddled him. I felt Apollonius behind me as I leaned down to lick Triarius' lips.

"Need you," I whispered. "Both of you..."

"Yes." Triarius slicked himself and pulled me up. I sat back and sank down onto his cock, moaning his name. "Lance."

"Fuck... God, you feel good..." Two slick fingers traced my stretched asshole and then pushed in slowly. I gasped and rested my head on Triarius' shoulder as Apollonius eased his fingers in deeper. "Oh, God. Fuck me... please..."

Apollonius kissed my shoulder, then leaned down further and kissed Triarius. His fingers never stopped moving, always sliding, stretching. The burn took my breath away, every stroke torturously gentle. I heard Triarius make a desperate noise and Apollonius pulled back to lick the blood from Triarius' lips. Then the fingers were gone and Apollonius nuzzled my neck.

"Ready?"

"God, yes." I tried not to freeze up when I felt his fingers withdraw, and I nearly shook apart when he started pushing his cock into my ass. "Yes!" I threw my head back and hissed, Triarius' nails digging into my thighs a sharp contrast to the exquisite pain. "Don't stop... fuck, don't stop..."

Soon as he was deep inside, Apollonius stilled and the three of us groaned. I'd never experienced anything like it, nothing nearly as intense as having two lovers inside me at once. They started moving slowly, alternating strokes, never leaving me empty. My brain shut down and I just rode them, the entire world tilting as they took turns pumping in and out of my ass. My orgasm surprised the hell out of me and I shouted, entire body jerking as come sprayed Triarius' stomach. Behind me, Apollonius grunted and thrust hard, growling out my name as his cock pulsed and throbbed inside me. Triarius didn't last long after and he held my hips pinned to his body, his back arching as he shot.

Dizzy, breathless, and deliciously sore, I collapsed on top of Triarius, barely aware when Apollonius pulled out. I felt two sets of arms slide around me and I fell asleep, perfectly content in my lovers' arms.

*Legends of the Romanorum, Book 6*
Dreams of Death

# Chapter Twenty-Eight

Aaron ditched his buddies easily enough. None of them had any clue what he was up to. If they did, they would have trailed him, then beat the ever-living shit out of him.

He'd left them trying to track Dracula and hadn't bothered to tell any of them he had a really good clue where the killer might strike next. He didn't think this person was a serial killer. No, it had to be an honest-to-God vampire. No matter what the speculation in the newspaper said.

With each victim, it had become easier and easier for the police to find them. The vampire was either getting exceptionally careless or, as Aaron suspected, increasingly panicked. The last victim had been found in a derelict building right outside of town. If Aaron's hunch was correct, the vampire wouldn't be too far off. The cops had no clue they were dealing with a real vampire. They were too busy with their killer profiling and lab reports.

No vampire in his right mind would commit these killings, not in this day and age of legal citizenship. It was far too easy to get a meal and maintain respectability for the vamps. Even the newspaper theorized it was a mortal trying to cause trouble for the vampires.

Making no effort to hide himself from anybody watching from derelict buildings, Aaron pushed open the old rusty gate of the rundown complex. The police had assumed since they hadn't found any signs of life in the surrounding area that the killer wasn't there. Aaron knew better. The vampire would be an expert at concealing himself from any searches, and the cops had no idea what they were really looking for. Chances were the vampire had the power to hide himself even if the cops were looking right at him. Other than the occasional breeze, everything was unusually still. The moon cast a silver-gray glow over the rubble-strewn ground, but the buildings themselves were hidden beneath shadows. It was the perfect place to hide, especially for a vampire.

He avoided the building where the yellow police tape flapped against the door. He doubted if the vampire would push his luck that much. Instead, he paused for a moment, looking over each building before he chose the one furthest from the others. It made a good place to start. Turning the knob, he found the door locked. Then he slowly circled the building, trying to find a way in.

"Bingo," he muttered to himself, seeing the broken window in the back wall. Raising himself up over the sill, he climbed into the window. He had to squirm to squeeze his way through the tight frame.

Once inside, he swung his flashlight, and the beam lit the broken wooden crates strewn over the floor. A rat scurried across the floor and darted into a hole in the wall. The air was stale, and dust particles drifted in the light as Aaron swept it around the room. The crates looked like pallets for stacking goods, and most were nothing more than enormous splinters now.

As he crept farther, he directed the light around the room. Looking towards one of the doors at the back, Aaron saw the flash of a shadow moving across the doorway. He lit the door, but there was nothing there. Aaron kept the flashlight steadily lighting the door. Beyond it was a hallway stretching on for what seemed like the entire length of the building. Doors led off from each side along the hall, and most were closed, their windows broken. Then the shadow reappeared in the hallway. It hovered a few yards in front of Aaron, but it didn't advance on him.

Aaron didn't move any closer to the strange darkness. "I know you're here, and I know what you are."

Though he probably should have been terrified, Aaron wasn't. He had something the vampire needed. And to get it, the vampire would have to let him live. His heartbeat accelerated.

Although the shadow didn't move, a deep, resonating voice broke the silence following Aaron's pronouncement.

"Who are you?"

"Aaron Sellers. Who are you?" Aaron lowered the flashlight out of courtesy.

"Taylor."

With the absence of the light, the shadow drifted closer. As it moved, it took on a more tangible form. The features were not clear, but from the shape, it was obvious this Taylor was a man.

"Why are you here?"

Aaron didn't retreat from the advancing form. Frowning slightly, he focused on trying to find details of a face within the misty dark. "I'm here because you need to get out of here. The cops are going to track you down and real soon. They aren't all stupid."

A laugh as dark as the blackness surrounding them was Taylor's immediate answer. "And what would you suggest? Given my nature, I am limited in my choices."

The tone of the laugh made Aaron shiver, yet he wasn't the least bit of afraid. Maybe a saner person would have been, but this was his dream come true. This town was too damn small to attract any vampires, and this was his only chance of seeing one.

"Not exactly." With a devious grin, Aaron fished in his jeans pocket and dug out his car keys. "I figured you had no way out of here. Your chariot awaits you, sir." After making an exaggerated bow, Aaron straightened, laughing. "I was right about you."

"Right about me?"

The figure stepped closer, and the shadows faded, revealing a fine-featured man who looked to be no more than in his late twenties. But his dark brown eyes held ages within them. He was dressed in black cloth pants and a white, loose shirt. His long, dark brown hair fell over his shoulders. The black boots he wore were as dusty and ragged as the rest of his clothing.

"How were you right about me?"

"You've been getting a bit panicky, Taylor." Nodding slowly, Aaron intently studied the man. Whoa. Yeah, he'd been expecting something in the region of good looking, but damn. Even in the shabby clothing, a certain quality showed through in the way Taylor held himself. The chiseled features gave the vampire a handsome, albeit arrogant, air. "I thought that you were getting nervous because the cops were starting to get closer and closer to you. And you can't get out of here without help."

Taylor's lips slowly curved in an odd smile. "A brave young man you are, to be propositioning me. Very well, Master Aaron

Sellers." Taylor bowed, though his gaze never left Aaron's. "You have piqued my curiosity."

"I didn't want them to catch you," Aaron said. "My car is outside, and I've got enough money to last for quite a while." He had cashed in every one of the bonds his grandparents had given him and sold about everything he owned except for the car to come up with the money.

One of Taylor's dark eyebrows rose at that. "You are intriguing." With that, Taylor walked by him, toward the window Aaron had used to come in.

"Uh, thanks." Aaron followed behind, studying the vampire's back. Excited thoughts ran through his head, along with a million and one questions. Finally, he settled on one. "How long were you asleep? This is 2028, by the way, just in case you didn't know."

"A hundred and twenty-two years," Taylor said as he slid effortlessly through the window. "And you, Master Sellers. How old are you?"

Aaron crawled out behind him, only he didn't have as easy of a time. Tumbling to the ground, he nearly cracked his head on a large rock. Scrambling up and brushing himself off, he answered, "I'm twenty-two. I'm willing to bet you have no idea of how the world has changed."

"Such beautiful youth," Taylor said with a grin. "Where might my chariot be?"

Aaron grimaced before he gestured to the other side of the building. "It's at the back gate. I didn't want anybody to see a car on the main street in front of this place." Pointing the flashlight towards the ground, Aaron led the way to the gate then out to his car. "The cops have found, like, six bodies so far. Any more out there?"

"No. I've not been out this evening." Dark eyes watched Aaron closely.

After closing the door behind him, Aaron went to the other side and got in. "Is it necessary for you to kill, Taylor?"

Taylor returned Aaron's look in silence for several seconds before answering. "I suppose not. Why?"

"Well, logically, if there are no dead bodies, there's nobody going to come looking for you. Ethically, you just can't kill." Aaron stayed to the back roads, driving in a meandering pattern. "Vampires are legal citizens now. No reason to kill. Not with people willing to line up for the privilege."

"Ethics were never my concern, but I am willing to feed without killing, if only to satisfy my curiosity. Where are we going?"

"Satisfy your curiosity about what? We're going to stop at a hotel so you can clean up, and I can get you some other clothes. I just want to make sure I wasn't noticed at the warehouse."

"I've never fed and not killed. I don't know how the beast inside me will react. There must be something to sate him." Taylor stared out the passenger side window as he spoke, his tone eerily conversational.

Aaron doubted if Taylor would try to kill him, at least for the moment. "You'll have to, Taylor, or you won't last long here. I'm sure you can tell things aren't like they were when you went to sleep."

"I have kept track of the pulse of part of this world, even in my rest."

As he drove out of town, Aaron didn't look back. He wanted to put some miles between them and New Vale before he stopped. "The nearest town is about twenty miles away, so it won't take more than fifteen minutes to get there."

"You've yet to tell me why you're helping me." Even in the dark, Taylor's stare was sharp and piercing as he looked over at Aaron.

"I told you: I didn't want them to catch you." Shrugging slightly, he met Taylor's look briefly. "I had a feeling what you were. It's like a dream for me to meet you. Well, one of your kind. You have no idea."

"A dream." Taylor's laugh was deep, even stronger in the enclosed area of the car. "What clued you in?"

"A group of friends and I have been following the killings. We knew everything going on. Enough of it leaked to the newspapers to label you Dracula. Nobody was serious about it. It was a hunch on our parts, and we didn't dismiss the real clues like the cops did. They just didn't want to believe anything that crazy. No vamp wants a death hunt on their ass."

"A following," Taylor mused. "Now that's interesting. Although, I must admit that I'm looking forward to a bath. And how do you suggest I feed?"

Pulling off onto the exit, Aaron stopped at the red light. "Find somebody to feed from and hope to God you don't kill them. I don't think I'm going to be much help to you if you leave a string of dead bodies everywhere we go."

"Then I will fuck when I feed," Taylor said matter-of-factly.

Any average person would have understood the concept of it being wrong to kill, but Aaron doubted very much it would work on Taylor. Getting that unexpected answer, Aaron stared at Taylor wide-eyed. "Umm, I suppose that would work?"

"It will have to." Taylor glanced back over at him, giving Aaron an odd smile.

Not quite sure what to make of it, Aaron looked away from him. When the light turned green, he pulled out onto the street and made a right. "We'll definitely have to get you cleaned up first. Unless you have some super-seductive powers or something."

"No one has ever turned me down."

"Okay. I'll take it that means yes." Aaron didn't doubt it at all. Even beneath the layer of dust and tattered clothing, Taylor's looks were astounding, and that was putting it mildly.

When he turned into the hotel parking lot, Aaron parked the car a bit away from the main entrance. "I'll get the room. It shouldn't take me more than a few minutes."

"I will be here."

# Chapter Twenty-Nine

After getting out of the car, Aaron headed into the hotel. He made sure they got a room in the back so hopefully nobody would see Taylor. Aaron really needed to get the man some clothing. He'd already guesstimated the man's size and planned to head over to the mall across the street while Taylor took a shower.

"We're in the back," he said once he got back into the car.

"My favorite place," Taylor said with a wink.

Aaron's eyes widened with the remark. What the hell did one say to that?

It only took a minute to pull into the back of the hotel to their room. "We're in 188." Looking quickly around, Aaron thankfully noted nobody seemed to be within sight.

As soon as they were in the room, Taylor studied it curiously. "A far cry from England."

"Modern convenience. What can I say?"

Aaron flipped on the TV. Taylor blinked at it, head tilted slightly. Aaron just chuckled. "Bathroom is back there, but I should probably show you how to use the tub, right?" Aaron wasn't quite sure just how modern the earlier 1900's had been.

"It might be helpful." Following Aaron to the bathroom, Taylor leaned against the doorframe, arms crossed over his chest.

As he spoke, Aaron pointed to the knobs. "Left is hot and right is cold. I'm thinking you might prefer a bath rather than a shower, so never mind about the middle button." Aaron started the water running for him. "You can change the temperature if you want to. There's soap and shampoo right on the edge."

Taylor slid past Aaron into the bathroom, brushing their bodies together lightly. Without another word, he began undressing, seemingly unmoved by Aaron still standing near.

Given the close quarters, Aaron tried to shift to get out of Taylor's way. While he would have enjoyed the sneak peek, he figured it wouldn't be too wise. "I'm going to head over to the store to get some clothes. It shouldn't take me too long." Grabbing his keys off of the TV, Aaron beat a hasty retreat out the door.

\* \* \*

Aaron returned to the hotel room in a relatively short time. He'd only bought a pair of jeans, a t-shirt, and underwear for Taylor. Opening the door, he stepped inside then quickly shut it behind him. The first thing he noticed was the magnificent body stretched out on the bed with only a towel around him. Try as he might, Aaron couldn't stop his gaze from slowly sweeping upward over Taylor.

"I'd forgotten how good it felt to sink into a tub of steaming water." Lying there on the bed, anyone else would have looked quite vulnerable in so little clothing. Taylor, however, looked predatory.

"You look a lot better without all the dirt." Acutely aware of Taylor's gaze following him, Aaron tossed the car keys on top of the TV, then moved towards the bed. As he stood at the edge, he dropped the shopping bag on the bed and pulled out the jeans and shirt. "I figured you could pick out whatever clothes you wanted later. So I just got these for you to go shopping in." Setting the shirt and pants down, he fished back into the bag and pulled out the package of underwear and socks, laying them near the rest of the clothes. "Last but not least, here's a pair of shoes. I think this stuff will fit, though it might be a little tight. You'll only have to wear it long enough to buy yourself some more clothes."

As Taylor sat up to reach for the clothes, his towel parted just enough to show the skin of his upper thigh. Lifting the shirt, he said, "I must thank you for this."

"You..." The word faded under Taylor's piercing look. Being bisexual, Aaron found the man beyond appealing. He just wasn't sure having a vampire lover would be a really good idea.

Oh, hell, who was he kidding? He'd fucking dreamed about it, but Taylor had an undeniably predatory air about him. Incredibly sexy, but downright dangerous as well.

"You're welcome. I've got enough money to cover us for a while. If I have to, I can get another job when we run out," Aaron rambled while trying to keep his attention on Taylor's face.

A slow smile crept across Taylor's lips, as if he knew exactly what Aaron was thinking. "I need to hunt."

"And not kill, right? Unless you want the cops to follow along wherever we go." Just a touch uncomfortable at Taylor's expression, Aaron picked up the smaller bag he'd put on the bed. Moving to the small fridge between the two beds, he opened it and put in the soda.

There came a sound of movement and then long fingers slid around Aaron's neck, caressing the nape. Pulling him back to stand up, Taylor brushed Aaron's hair away and whispered,

"Why have you not asked what it feels like? I know that's what you want, what you've dreamed about for so long."

Startled, a small, nervous sound emerged from Aaron's throat. "I... I just met you, ya know." Though he should have pulled away, Aaron didn't. The oddest sensation tingled along his skin where Taylor's fingers touched him.

Taylor's breath was warm when he laughed low. "You don't lie well, Aaron." He bent his head and gave the side of Aaron's throat a little nip—without breaking the skin—then released him to get dressed.

When Taylor moved away from him, it surprised the hell out of Aaron. He'd been sure the vampire would bite him. He wasn't sure if he felt relieved or disappointed. "You still haven't told me if you're not going to kill." He turned to glance at Taylor.

The towel dropped, revealing muscular thighs and a tight ass. "I told you I would give it a try," Taylor said over his shoulder. "Though that's going to require finding a man who doesn't mind having two sharp teeth piercing his throat when he comes."

Taylor's comments sent Aaron into a coughing fit as he seriously tried to clear the images out of his head. When he could finally speak, he tried to sound as casual as possible. "That shouldn't be too much of a problem if you look in the right area. This place has a couple of gay bars. I hope you can make them forget afterwards, though."

"I can." Taylor bent over to pick up the jeans, leaving the underwear on the bed. "I can blanket a mind until nothing exists but pleasure if need be."

"Good, because we don't need a bunch people running around telling tales about you." Relieved, he leaned down to open the fridge and got one of the sodas. Settling on the edge of the bed, he tried to avoid Taylor. The man seemed to have no problem running around naked with him in the room. Aaron had the feeling he was in for a hell of a time. "Did you want me to go along with you?"

"You are most welcome to." Taylor zipped up the pants and chuckled. "You weren't kidding about them being tight, but it's nothing I'm not used to."

How could Aaron not look down? As his gaze fastened on the front of Taylor's pants, he noticed the obvious bulge of fabric. "Umm, yeah. Tight." Clearing his throat, he continued, "I know where the gay bars in town are. So I better go along anyway."

Aaron took a quick drink before standing to get the car keys. Before he could get past Taylor, however, the vampire spun, his arm sliding around Aaron's waist and pulling him right up against his muscular body in one smooth motion.

"Then again, perhaps I do not need to hunt."

"Oh, fuck." Before Aaron could think, the words came out. His hands ended up against the hard lines of Taylor's chest. Whether to push him back or touch him, Aaron wasn't sure. He didn't push, though; he just stared up into the dark eyes, mesmerized. He opened his mouth to say something, but nothing would come out except a soft whimper.

"That's the idea, is it not?" Taylor smiled, his fangs dropping slowly.

Whatever he'd been going to say flew clear out of his head as he saw the sharp white tips. Unable to suppress his shiver, it shot through him like lightning. Yeah, he'd dreamed of what it would be like. To be fed from, knowing your blood sustained the life of another. In a split second, Aaron knew Taylor would bite him. It occurred to him he should struggle, but he didn't. "No killing, right?"

"No killing," Taylor whispered as he lowered his head, licking Aaron's lips slowly.

Should he trust Taylor? Probably not, but Aaron really couldn't think. With the touch, Aaron wanted a kiss. Oh, hell, he wanted more. He could feel the slight dig of Taylor's cock, and a low moan rose in his throat with the brush of their lips.

Smiling against Aaron's mouth, Taylor parted Aaron's lips with his tongue, drowning out all other sounds as his mouth covered Aaron's. His other hand slid through Aaron's hair, cupping the back of his head. With a slight shift, Taylor deepened the kiss, a low sound—almost like a growl—filling Aaron's mouth.

Aaron didn't stop any of it. His hands slid up over Taylor's chest then encircled his neck as Aaron arched against him. Mouth tightening to the invasion, Aaron let Taylor kiss him.

Breaking slowly away, Taylor tipped Aaron's head back, tracing a path with his tongue down the arch of Aaron's throat. "I will fuck you when I feed," he said, his breath hot against Aaron's skin.

The pronouncement didn't startle Aaron. The way Taylor had a hold of him, he sort of expected they'd end up on one of the beds. Breath escaping him in a soft hiss, he only got out one word: "Yes."

Taylor growled and nipped at Aaron's throat as he worked first his jeans, and then Aaron's open. "Get them off. I want skin."

Aaron quickly shoved his jeans over his hips, then took off his underwear. After kicking them off, he pulled his shirt over his head. He watched Taylor, wanting to see the whole package and not just the back half. A low groan escaped Aaron as he slipped to his knees in front of Taylor. Licking his lips, he reached for Taylor's cock. He leaned forward, tongue tasting the glistening drops at the slit.

A low, rumbling groan rolled through Taylor and his hands fell to Aaron's head. "Yes," he hissed, hips pushing forward. "Open your mouth for me."

Aaron caught the heated flare lighting the vampire's eyes as his mouth engulfed the hard flesh. He hummed, the vibration surrounding Taylor's cock, and Aaron tightened his lips, taking the man's cock to the root.

As the leisurely strokes increased, Taylor's fingers tightened on Aaron's head. His cock flexed over Aaron's tongue as he pumped in and out of Aaron's mouth. "Enough," he growled a few moments later, pulling Aaron to his feet. "On the bed. Now."

Aaron stood and moved to his pack. Unzipping the side pocket, he pulled out a tube of lube before he went straight to the bed. Kneeling on the covers, he looked back over his shoulder at Taylor. "On my back or on my knees?"

Taylor stared at him for a moment, tongue wetting his lips while he stroked his cock. "Your back. Ready yourself for me."

Aaron rolled to his back and opened the lube to squirt some on his fingers. Then he reached between his legs and slipped a finger inside. He placed his feet flat on the bed and arched up slightly towards Taylor. His breath hitched in his throat as he added another finger, slicking himself. Aaron could never do this for long without wanting a hell of a lot more.

"Yes," Taylor said, kneeling on the bed between Aaron's legs. Bracing himself on one hand by Aaron's head, he hovered over Aaron. His gaze never left Aaron's and he grinned slowly, baring his fangs. "More. Open yourself. I want to hear you beg for me."

Excitement stirred through Aaron with the look trained on him. Pushing his fingers as deeply into himself as he could, each twist sent his own need sharply skyrocketing. "Please, Taylor. Let me feel you. Now. Please." He didn't care that he was begging. Aaron needed to feel Taylor's cock, and just as badly wanted the vampire to bite him.

Taylor's eyes went from brown to red and he pulled Aaron's hand away. Grabbing both wrists, he pinned Aaron's hands above his head. With little ceremony, he was inside Aaron, his mouth crashing down on Aaron's as he surged deep.

Instead of trying to get away from the suddenly painful penetration, Aaron arced hard against Taylor. Each feeling blended as Taylor held him down and filled his ass. His nails dug into Taylor, trying to free his hands to reach the vampire.

Breaking away from the kiss, Taylor took Aaron over and over. His hold on Aaron's wrists tightened, and Aaron couldn't look away from those mesmerizing eyes.

"Come on," Taylor grunted. "Show me how much you want to come."

Aaron had never been taken in such a brutal way, yet his body wanted it. The tug of his hands became more frantic in an effort to reach Taylor. In the vampire's eyes, he could see darkness, and it sent a thread of panic through Aaron. He tried to speak, but no words would come out. Only the rising sound in his throat answered Taylor as Aaron writhed beneath him.

With a sound that greatly resembled a roar, Taylor buried himself deep inside Aaron. The strike was swift, his fangs piercing Aaron's throat as he filled Aaron's body with his seed.

The pain increased tenfold, and Aaron's body convulsed. In his mind, it became one with the pleasure sweeping over him as he came with a scream. It relentlessly dragged his senses and body down with it in a spiraling black void while Taylor fed from him. Inside, fear crept in, not knowing if the vampire would stop. As he shook, Aaron tried to struggle, but Taylor's hold on him kept him powerless.

# Chapter Thirty

Taylor's low, dark laugh broke through the growing darkness. *The line between life and death is a fine one to tread. You are in no danger of falling. Come back to me.*

Aaron clung to the voice inside his head as he surfaced from the near blackout. It took him several seconds to even feel his body again. *Oh fuck, I'm sore.*

Opening his eyes, he blinked quickly when he saw Taylor wasn't on top of him anymore. The vampire was on his side, staring down at Aaron with an infernal grin. "What the..."

"Welcome back," Taylor said, grin widening. "Was it what you'd always hoped it would be?"

Aaron wasn't sure if he should get out of the bed and run or beg for more. His entire body ached with the reminder of what Taylor had done to him. "Beyond that."

Taylor chuckled softly. "I can assure you that it isn't always like that."

He'd never realized he was such a pain slut, either. To Aaron, it had almost seemed as if he couldn't get enough, and that confused the hell out of him. "Good, because I'm not sure I could handle something like that all the time."

Taylor smoothed his fingertip over Aaron's lips in a gentle caress. "I will only need to feed once a week now."

Finally capable of movement, Aaron twisted towards the vampire. A grunt escaped him when twinges rippled through his body. "Once a week I can handle. I think." When Aaron realized the vampire might want someone else as well, he added, "I mean, if you don't need somebody else or something."

"I must admit that having one person around is convenient," Taylor said with a wink. "And I'm not about to complain about the sex."

The vampire appeared to be more relaxed and easygoing. Aaron felt as if he might have caught a glimpse of something more than just a predatory creature. "I don't think I can complain. I'm starting to think I like pain or something."

Taylor's smile was positively wicked. "I'll remember that."

Hesitantly, Aaron's fingers smoothed over the vampire's chest. "Am I going to regret mentioning it?" Aaron couldn't quite hide his own curiosity about how much pain he could take, and how much pleasure it would bring.

Catching Aaron's fingers, Taylor drew them to his lips. "I promise nothing but pain and pleasure," he murmured, tongue sliding out to lick Aaron's skin.

* * *

Aaron had been keeping an eye on the news for any further mentions of the mystery killings. Thankfully, the more distance they put between them and New Vale, the less the news focused on the unusual killings.

Once they crossed into Colorado, Aaron relaxed considerably. Deciding to take a break early, they stopped in Colorado Springs at the base of the Rockies. After paying for the hotel room, Aaron drove to the back of the building and parked the car in front of Room 164.

Taylor got out and breathed deep, even though he didn't need to. "Very nice." He threw Aaron a wicked smile before closing the car door.

"Can't wait to get into the mountains tomorrow. Used to vacation every summer at my parents' cabin near Gunnison. Wait until you see it." Following behind Taylor, Aaron passed him to unlock the hotel door and flick on the light. The room appeared to be pretty much like any other hotel room.

Taylor was suddenly behind him, crowding Aaron into the room, the door closing on its own with a click. "I," he said, hands gripping Aaron's shoulders as he lowered his head to nick Aaron's neck with his fangs, "can't wait to get into you."

Aaron leaned heavily back against him. A shiver coursed through his body and his hand crept up into Taylor's hair. He wanted nothing more than the pain and pleasure Taylor would give him. "Anything, Taylor, anything."

"Undress," Taylor whispered. The word might have been softly spoken, but behind it there was a clear command.

Though Aaron hadn't clearly thought about how things were between them, he obediently began pulling his shirt off over his head. As he slowly turned to face the vampire, he ran his hands down his own chest, caressing over the skin. Stepping backwards towards the bed, he lowered his hands to slide his shorts down over his hips and kick off his sneakers.

Taylor stalked him—actually stalked him—across the room. "Turn around and face the wall, hands flat and legs spread."

At times, Taylor exuded an eerie predatory hunger, from the dark, hooded eyes to the seamlessly smooth movement of his body. Every time, it sharply reminded Aaron how potentially dangerous Taylor could be. A tingling of fear ran through Aaron as he faced the wall, hands against it and his legs wide apart.

The sound of clothes dropping to the floor followed and Taylor pressed close, cock hard and thick, nestling against the crack of Aaron's ass. "Such a sweet ass you have," he purred. One hand cupped Aaron's right buttock. "I look forward to testing it." Without warning, Taylor stepped back, and the palm of his hand landed a sharp, hard smack to Aaron's ass.

The surprise whack made Aaron jump and he turned his head to look at the vampire. A tingling heat followed in the wake, surprising Aaron even more.

Another slap quickly followed, Taylor's smile unnerving, wicked. He smoothed his palm on the abused flesh—the touch cool, soothing. "You mark so well."

Aaron found himself unexpectedly arching his ass back towards Taylor with the alternating sensations of pain and caress. His gaze held Taylor's questioningly.

"Mm, you like that, do you?" The vampire moved away and sat down on the edge of the bed. Then he patted his legs. "Over my legs. Hands flat on the floor."

Aaron turned away from the wall and moved towards Taylor. Draping his body over the vampire's legs, he placed his hands flat on the floor. He never really stopped and thought about why he obeyed Taylor or even noticed the control the vampire effectively exerted over him.

One hand resting lightly on the small of Aaron's back, Taylor spread Aaron's legs with the other. "Such a pretty ass, nice tight hole..." His fingertip skated over the puckered hole, pressing but not penetrating.

Aaron willingly spread his legs, and the play of Taylor's finger made him squirm. The position felt somewhat awkward to him, but he momentarily forgot that with the ghosting touch.

Taylor gave a dark chuckle, then the hand was gone. "Count." It was the only warning Aaron had before the first strike landed across the crease of his ass, just above his hole.

Startled, Aaron jumped slightly, not entirely certain what to expect. It wasn't until a moment stretched by in silence before he actually got out the word. "One."

Another sharp smack landed on his right buttock, with Taylor's hand pressing into his skin, the heat tangible.

"Two." This time Aaron answered more quickly, though his voice held a surprised tone. It had never occurred to him that he might actually like this. The arch of his ass lifted slightly in anticipation of the next strike before he tried to still himself.

Taylor's prick was hard beneath him, pressing into Aaron. He smacked Aaron's left buttock, the sound louder, the sting sharper. Then he gave the right one a hard slap.

It hurt like hell, and Aaron forgot to count. He closed his eyes, and his cock rubbed against Taylor's leg. Biting at his lip, Aaron stopped the moan that wanted out.

"You're not counting, pet." Several more hard slaps to his ass, far from light and gentle, followed Taylor's words.

"Shit!" Aaron struggled to keep up with each hit through the increased squirming of his hips against Taylor's lap. "Five, six, seven..." His ass burned to the point that tears formed in the corner of his eyes, and Aaron struggled to keep up. "Eight."

Taylor slid his other hand lower and spread the cheeks of Aaron's ass apart. The light touch of his finger drifted over the puckered hole before Taylor tapped it with his fingers none too gently.

Aaron opened himself to the level of pain Taylor offered and only wanted more. A rough upward jerk of his ass nudged to Taylor's fingers, though he didn't know what he begged for. "Taylor, please."

"Please... what?" Taylor asked, tapping Aaron's hole again. "What shall I do now that I have your attention, pet? Bend you over the bed and fuck you? Mark this sweet ass until you're in tears and begging me to stop... or for more?"

"More. Fuck me," Aaron gasped out, wanting it all. The strangest need surged through him, and he couldn't control it.

With inhuman strength, Taylor twisted and shoved Aaron down onto the bed, Aaron's knees on the floor. Then came the sound of a zipper and the pop of a cap. Two fingers were swiftly buried deep inside Aaron, twisting until Taylor nailed his prostate, stroking and rubbing. The blanket muffled Aaron's cries, and his legs spread wider for Taylor. The rub of the fingers sent shudders through Aaron, and he fucked himself on the vampire's fingers.

"More, pet?" Taylor added a third finger, scissoring them all apart, stretching Aaron open. His other palm connected to Aaron's right ass cheek in a hard, sharp slap.

"Yes," Aaron answered him with one short, hissed word. The pain and pleasure melded into one in Aaron's brain, making him crave them both. The burning stretch in his ass caused Aaron to grind against the bed for more friction against his cock.

Taylor slicked his cock and knelt behind Aaron. Then he pushed three fingers of his other hand inside Aaron and spread him wide open. "Yes," he growled, thrusting his cock into Aaron, fingers still keeping him stretched.

Aaron's fingers clenched tightly to the covers beneath him and only the bed muffled his scream with the sudden brutal invasion.

Taylor pulled his fingers out and gripped Aaron's hips, nails lengthening, slicing into Aaron's flesh. "So hot and tight," he hissed. "I can smell your need." He shoved his cock deep, hips jarring against Aaron's ass. "I can hear the blood in your veins, your pulse calling to me."

"Hurt me. Want you to hurt me." Aaron craved Taylor's assault on his body. Each sensation of pain merged with the tension of arousal surging through him. Baring his throat to the vampire, he invited even more.

Taylor snarled and struck, fangs driving deep into Aaron's throat, his jaw clamping tightly. He drank deep as he fucked Aaron, keeping the rhythm brutal, unrelenting. Nails became claws, piercing Aaron's skin, digging in to hold him. When Taylor came, the growl that accompanied it was vicious, bloodthirsty.

The massive overload tightened Aaron's muscles when it swept through him in a drenching flood. With repeated spasms Aaron came as he screamed mindlessly, totally lost in the pain and pleasure ravaging him.

Taylor didn't stop even and the pull on Aaron's neck was strong, forcing his orgasm to last well beyond the normal limits. Only when Aaron's heart began to slow did Taylor pull away, easing out of Aaron's body and laying him gently on the bed.

"Aaron..." Taylor slit his own wrist and pressed it to Aaron's lips. "Drink. It will heal you."

Feeling the weakness taking him over, Aaron could only lie limply on the bed, drowning in the lingering aftereffects. He tried to focus on the vampire, his tongue darting out to taste the blood on his lips. Not knowing why, he instantly fastened his mouth on the wound to take what he could. As he drank, Aaron could feel the oddest rush through his body and somehow his mind seemed to open. Staring at Taylor, an overwhelming barrage of images and knowledge struck him out of nowhere.

"You belong to me now, Aaron," Taylor told him, though it seemed as if the vampire's voice was distant, somewhere deep inside his mind.

# Chapter Thirty-One

Aaron could feel a hunger he'd never experienced before as he drank from Taylor. Everything hit him in a rush, and his mind couldn't scramble fast enough to keep up with it. It took long moments before he finally released Taylor's wrist. Lifting his head, he glanced down at himself and actually saw the marks on his body beginning to heal.

"Come. I'm sure security has been alerted to our activities." Taylor helped Aaron up slowly, then led him into the bathroom. Keeping one arm around Aaron's waist, Taylor leaned over and started the shower.

Since Aaron could barely remember everything that had happened, he wasn't sure about Taylor's comment. Still, he stepped into the shower and quickly had to hold to the wall to keep steady. Grabbing at the soap with his free hand, Aaron began to wash off under the hot spray.

"I'm going to do something about the mess," Taylor said, stroking Aaron's back before closing the curtain.

\* \* \*

It took Taylor only a few minutes to deal with the top sheet on the bed. There hadn't been too much blood spilled. Still, the less there was visible, the better. He remade the bed as quickly as possible, taking great care to cover the sheet. The moment he finished tucking the blankets in, there came a hard knock on the door.

Taylor pulled on his pants and went to answer it, blinking at the parking lot light shining in his eyes. "Can I help you gentlemen?"

Two hotel security men stood outside the door, both eyeing Taylor with suspicion. "We got a report of screaming heard from this room. We're here to investigate."

Without another word, the other man pushed forward to open the door further. "You want to tell us what's going on?"

A moment later, Aaron came out of the bathroom with a towel wrapped around him. Seeing the security, he gave them a puzzled look, "What's going on?"

"That's precisely what we're here to find out," one of the men said.

"I do apologize for any disturbances." Taylor held out a hand to Aaron. "My lover, he enjoys a bit of pain with his pleasure. I am not one to deny him that."

"Oh, shit." Aaron turned beet red, and his gaze flew between the two men and Taylor. "I was too loud."

One of the men gave him a disgusted look before he poked nosily around the room, then went into the bathroom. The other man looked like he was trying not to laugh. When the guard couldn't find anything suspicious, he returned to the main room. "Didn't find anything."

With a shake of his head the second guard commented, "Keep it down in here, all right?"

"Yes, sir," Taylor said with a graceful nod. "Once again, we apologize for the disturbance." He saw the men out, closing and locking the door behind them. Then he turned to Aaron and chuckled.

"Oh, man, that's embarrassing," Aaron muttered, moving towards the bed. "Didn't realize I got that loud."

Taylor snaked his arms around Aaron's waist and placed a soft kiss on his neck. "I, for one, am not complaining. How are you feeling?"

If anything, Aaron seemed even more confused. "I remember hurting, but there's no mark on me. Did you..."

"Did I... turn you?" Taylor whispered, breath hot over Aaron's skin. "No, I did not. Though you are now my ghoul, Aaron. You could survive without my blood, but it would be painful, eventually driving you insane if you were to be denied."

"Your blood. I can smell it."

"Give it time, pet. It's a lot to process." Taylor turned Aaron around and sat him down on the bed, settling beside him. "There is much to explain, Aaron. We are bound now. Nothing can change that. Because of my blood, you will heal faster and live longer. You will no longer age as other humans do."

"Bound? I don't think that bothers me at all. The rest means I'm sort of like you, but not. I think I understand that."

\* \* \*

Aaron had been aware of his own growing need for the vampire. It wasn't like it snuck up on him all of a sudden. In retrospect, Aaron had the feeling it was what he wanted all along.

"You're taking this awfully well," Taylor mused. "I would not have done it without your permission, but in the height of passion, I took too much from you. I'm not ready to give you up."

Reaching for Taylor's hand, Aaron drew it to his lips, pressing several kisses to it. "Probably because I was hoping I would mean something to you. I think I've been praying for that since I first saw you."

Taylor withdrew his hand and made a small cut on his neck, then pulled Aaron close. "Then drink," he murmured.

The sudden sharp increase in the scent of Taylor's blood pulled a low moan from Aaron. He nuzzled the vampire's throat, tongue licking at the sweet drops. With a twist, Aaron pushed Taylor back to the bed to quickly straddle him and his mouth fastened hungrily on the wound.

"Yes..." The word was growled, drawn out, Taylor's hands clutching Aaron's hips, his body arching. "Aaron..."

The possessive tone of Taylor's voice came though loud and clear. The vampire considered Aaron to be his, and nothing in Aaron argued against it. Instead, he drew small mouthfuls of Taylor's blood to appease a near insatiable need inside him. With his hands and body, Aaron kept Taylor pinned. After a long moment, he released the hungry hold on Taylor long enough to whisper, "Have to be yours."

"You are mine." Taylor kissed a slow path from Aaron's ear to his throat, licking. "For eternity."

Burying his face against Taylor's throat, Aaron tried to hide the forming tears in his eyes. Never in his life had he truly dreamed he would have what Taylor offered him. The need and craving were damn near overwhelming. He'd never been anyone's before, never thought he would be.

"Shh..." Taylor stroked his hands over Aaron's back. "Come back home with me, back to England."

Startled by the request, Aaron lifted his head quickly. "England?"

"I don't belong here," Taylor said quietly. "*We* don't belong here. My home is in England. Or was. That is neither here nor there, as I will find us a place."

"If that's what you want, then that's what we'll do. We'll need to settle here for a short time while we try to get identification for you." Aaron would follow wherever Taylor led him.

"Nonsense. Some friendships never die; I have ways of getting us there unknown."

"Then I guess I'll let you handle it." Though he wasn't sure of what Taylor was talking about, Aaron agreed anyway.

"Do you trust me?"

Aaron didn't hesitate. "Yeah, I do, Taylor."

"Good, then we will leave come nightfall tomorrow. For now..." Taylor's grin widened and he shifted, legs moving out from under Aaron and wrapping around him. "I have a need of my own..."

After tugging the towel from around him, Aaron threw it to the floor and his hips deliberately pressed downward against Taylor. "What need? You have only to ask, and I'll do anything you want."

"Fuck me," Taylor whispered in Aaron's ear.

The vampire's voice and words sent a distinct throb straight through to Aaron's cock and drew a low groan from him. Turning his head, he nipped sharply at Taylor's ear. "Anything you want."

Taylor groaned and worked a hand between them, unfastening his pants. He managed to get them down and off, then gripped Aaron's hips, pushing up to slide their cocks together. "Yes... pet... in me."

Aaron slipped a hand down to stroke slowly over both of them, strengthening the building arousal. He lengthened the moment of anticipation with each tight slide of his fist around their cocks. The nip of his teeth and flicks of his tongue left a trail on Taylor's skin along the line of his throat.

Taylor rumbled, hips pushing up. "Need you, Aaron... now... deep..."

After quickly preparing himself, Aaron shifted slightly lower, pushing the length of his cock along Taylor's ass. Desire raced through him when he first felt the velvet heat swallowing him. When he was buried tightly inside the vampire, Aaron's lips caught Taylor's, silencing any sound with the hungry probe of his tongue.

Hips jerking upward, Taylor fisted his hands in Aaron's hair, growls filling the kiss. He rocked his hips, driving Aaron deeper. *"Take me..."*

Fierce need rolled through Aaron, driving him harder and tighter in against Taylor. One hand returned to play over the vampire's cock as the other used the bed for support. The hungry lick of his tongue repeatedly delved into Taylor's mouth. He became connected to his vampire lover, his thoughts pulling at Taylor as demandingly as his thrusts.

Taylor tore away from the kiss and arched his neck, a cut appearing. "Now!"

Aaron's teeth fastened to the wound, drinking heavily from him. With each shudder of his body, the edge of his teeth bit harder into Taylor's flesh.

Fingers fisted in Aaron's hair, Taylor cried out, shuddering hard as he came. He bucked and writhed beneath Aaron, heat pouring over Aaron's fingers. The jerk of his hips demanded Aaron's release as well. The hard strain of Aaron's body kept him tightly within Taylor as he came on the heels of the vampire's climax. Drawing back his head, Aaron kissed his lover, sharing the taste of his blood.

Taylor hummed, hands easing their hold as he cupped Aaron's face. "So beautiful," he whispered.

For a brief moment, Aaron could feel a nearly incomprehensible flood of thoughts and feelings from Taylor. It felt as if the vampire was trying to stake claim on him in a way Aaron couldn't fully understand. Bewildered, he opened his eyes and stared down at Taylor.

Blinking up at him, Taylor opened his mouth to speak, then closed it again. "Aaron... I..."

Shaking his head, Aaron didn't say anything for a long moment. His own previous notions of Taylor being some sort of fantasy vampire figure had just been blown all to hell. The vampire's life had been laid bare to him; Aaron struggled to keep up with the influx of knowledge and images, and beneath that a slow, rising understanding began to form. Intensely complicated, everything wasn't as cut and dried as a fantasy.

A fingertip silenced Taylor, and Aaron whispered, "I understand, and I don't. But I'm trying."

Taylor nodded and closed his eyes. "I know."

For the first time, Aaron realized there were many things to fear in Taylor, and he couldn't comprehend all of it. The rush of his own thoughts was too hard to still, yet he tried desperately to push it away. Laying his head on Taylor's chest, he took in several deep breaths.

The vampire stroked his hair and back, the touch soothing. "I'm not as perfect as the vampires of fantasy are," Taylor said quietly. "I have my faults, but I promise you that I will protect you."

"Why wouldn't you kill me, Taylor? There's no earthly reason you wouldn't." Aaron closed his eyes, more confused than ever about his position in all of this. Something he willingly undertook, yet he'd be the first to acknowledge that he obviously had had no clue at all.

Taylor sighed and rolled them, Aaron slipping out of him. Propping himself on his elbow, the vampire studied Aaron in silence for a moment before speaking. "You are right—there is no reason. But what would I gain if I did? The need to hunt again? More loneliness?" Taylor shook his head. "I think not. I find that I'm quite fond of you, and given that you are my ghoul now, you have no choice but to remain with me. I don't plan on letting you go."

Aaron caught the irony of his own situation, but his sense of humor simply wasn't up to it.

"I guess I'm in for the long haul." Rolling to his back, Aaron sprawled out, staring up at the ceiling. His mind had pretty much shut down, making it easy for him to act more casually. "When did you want to leave here?"

"Sleep now," Taylor murmured, pressing a soft kiss to Aaron's lips. "The sun will be up soon, and we will need the rest."

Obedient to the words, Aaron closed his eyes before he rolled back over to nestle against Taylor. His breath escaped him in a quiet sigh, warming over Taylor's skin.

# Chapter Thirty-Two

*A few days later, at an undisclosed port in England...*

"Can I help you?" The old man on the dock stopped his work and eyed Taylor and Aaron suspiciously.

Taylor walked up to him and whispered, "I'm looking for Alex Davis."

"Master Taylor," the man muttered. "Yes, of course. Right this way."

Nodding, Taylor took Aaron's hand and they fell into step behind the old man. Gazing inquisitively at Taylor, Aaron waited for an explanation. When one wasn't forthcoming, he asked quietly, "You planning on telling me what's going on? You've been quiet since we boarded that ship."

"I'm part of a brotherhood, if you will, of others like me," Taylor explained, his voice low. "A council of elders, so to speak. A name can carry weight." He looked over at Aaron. "Never forget that, should we ever be separated."

"That's what all of this secretiveness is about?"

"Yes. It's something we are sworn to protect—the identities of those within the brotherhood, and the existence of the brotherhood itself."

Aaron didn't say anything for a very long time. He simply glanced at the back of the other man then at Taylor before they got into a waiting car. He really wasn't sure what he'd gotten himself into. When it was just him and Taylor, it didn't seem quite so sinister.

No one said a word as the old man closed the door. There was a black glass window between the back seat and the front.

All other windows were just as dark, throwing them into pitch blackness. The car pulled off and Taylor let go of Aaron's hand, slipping an arm around Aaron's shoulders.

"There is nothing to fear."

Having his own reservation about that, Aaron just kept quiet, though he shifted in against Taylor's side. He'd never been in a car with this much tinting, and it really didn't help. "Where are we going?"

"To see an old friend. I trust Alex. He is the one with whom I arranged this. We'll be staying in his home for as long as need be. My keep is no longer standing."

"Your keep?" A long silenced followed before Aaron spoke again. "There's a lot you didn't tell me."

"Yes. My family home was destroyed long ago. I imagine the ruins are still there."

"How long are we going to be at Alex's place? Then where are we going?"

"We'll be there as long as we need to be, until I can procure another place for us."

Aaron wasn't sure how much time had passed before the car stopped. He remained silent beside Taylor as the door opened, then followed Taylor as he got out.

"Welcome to Davis Manor," Taylor said as he held out a hand to Aaron.

Looking up at the large Tudor style mansion, Aaron nodded.

"Come. Our room is ready. We will meet with Alex later." Taylor bypassed the main door and led Aaron to a smaller side entrance. Pushing open the heavy wooden door, he stepped into the small entryway. Once the door was closed, he cupped

Aaron's face, forcing Aaron to look only at him. "I know this is new but please understand that I will never let harm come to you, Aaron."

"I know. I just never realized there was all of this. Like it's all secret. I thought it was just me and you."

"It will always be only us." Taylor pulled Aaron close, lips claiming Aaron's in a kiss.

He relaxed slightly with Taylor's reassurance. Slipping his arms around Taylor's neck, Aaron leaned against him, enjoying the distraction. Aaron felt like he was becoming impossibly attached to Taylor, and still wasn't fully sure where he fit into all of this. Taylor's tongue swept through his mouth—devouring, possessing. The pressure grew stronger, insistent.

Lost in his own emotional and physical responses to Taylor, Aaron clung to him, giving into the demand of Taylor's kiss. His fingers clutched tightly at Taylor's shirt and in his hair, holding him for support. Taylor started backing Aaron up until Aaron was against a wall.

"Want you," he whispered, pushing his thigh between Aaron's legs.

"You have everything of me, Taylor." He ground tightly to Taylor's thigh, and a pained groan of need slipped free. His head tipped back against the wall, and he stared at his lover, feeling the betrayal of arousal of his own body.

"Need to taste you, Aaron..." Taylor slid to his knees, fingers deftly working Aaron's pants open.

Aaron's hand followed him down, resting on his head as Taylor tugged at his pants. Seeing his lover on his knees in front of him did all sorts of funny things to Aaron's insides. His other hand impatiently tugged back the material of his pants.

Once Aaron's cock was freed, Taylor breathed in deep. He gripped Aaron's cock around the base and licked the clear drops from the tip. Try as he might, Aaron couldn't still the impatient nudge of his hips, seeking the wet warmth of Taylor's mouth.

"Sweet..." Whatever else Aaron had meant to say was lost in a gasp of breath. With a demanding push, his cock slid further between Taylor's lips. A more urgent need arose, and Aaron began fucking Taylor's mouth. Just the sight of his cock disappearing into the vampire's throat sent a trembling through his entire body.

Taylor reached up with both hands and slid them beneath Aaron's shirt to pinch and twist his nipples. His lips tightened around Aaron's cock, and he swallowed, lips touching the curls at the base. The sensation bolted like lightening up Aaron's spine and he groaned, whispering Taylor's name. Several long thrusts filled Taylor's mouth, and each strengthened the urge riding Aaron's body. Full realization hit Aaron as he came, spurting inside Taylor's mouth. Instantly his mind and body were lost in the overwhelming blend.

Groaning, Taylor licked him clean and pulled off slowly. One hand dropped to Taylor's lap, and he pressed the heel of his hand against his cock, still trapped in his pants. "Need you..."

Quickly refastening his pants, he dropped to his knees in front of Taylor. More than eager to return the favor, Aaron yanked Taylor's pants open.

"Aaron." Hands on Aaron's head, Taylor pushed him down, hips thrusting upward the moment his cock was free. "Please..."

Sliding down, Aaron stretched out, mouth quickly engulfing Taylor's cock in a hungry pressure. Lips and tongue worked quickly over him, suckling on the hard flesh each time it pushed into his mouth.

Gasping, Taylor thrust up, pushing his cock into Aaron's throat. "Yes..."

The tightness of his lips slid over Taylor's cock, tongue pressing against the underside. As his throat relaxed, Aaron took him fully in, sucking on the hard flesh eagerly.

Taylor let out a deep growl, hips jerking in response. "Aaron!" Heat pumped into Aaron's mouth, Taylor's fingers fisting tight in Aaron's hair. Aaron's mouth worked around him, swallowing the thick liquid hungrily.

With a groan, Taylor slumped onto the floor. "Damn..."

Chuckling, Aaron quickly refastened Taylor's pants. "You know how much I love doing that for you."

"By all means, don't ever stop."

Aaron abruptly looked away from Taylor. "Come on, we better get to our room before somebody comes out here." Although he knew Taylor wasn't stupid, but Aaron wasn't going to press the issue. Not yet, anyway.

Taylor got up and took Aaron's hand. "This way," he said as he led Aaron down a dark hallway.

"How long will we be staying here?"

Taylor made an abrupt left turn and started up a set of winding stone steps. "I don't know." When they reached the top, he pressed on what appeared to be a wall. The stone slid away, opening into a large bedroom.

When he stepped into the room, Aaron felt like he entered the past. The huge, antique four-poster bed was lavishly carved, and every piece of furniture was clearly very old. An understated elegance and wealth cried out in each piece. If anything, it only reminded Aaron just how much he wasn't really a part of Taylor's life.

Without letting go, Taylor tugged Aaron toward the bed. "Sit. We need to talk."

"About?" Aaron settled beside him then laid back on the bed, dangling his feet over the edge.

Taylor sighed and raked his fingers through his hair. "I haven't been with anyone in ages who makes me want to go back on the vows I've made. But you..." He looked over at Aaron. "For you, I would do it."

Not sure what Taylor was talking about, Aaron gave him a puzzled look. "What vow?"

"Aaron, I am part of a brotherhood. We were branded as murderers by our own kind. While the majority have sworn to preserve human life—my brotherhood has vowed to use it. We are not the romantic figures that others portray us to be. We are monsters. You've seen that, with me. One of my vows was to maintain the balance of power—to never turn a human, as mortals are seen as weak, as cattle. Yet I can't help but hope that maybe one day, you will want to be a part of my world, of whatever life it is that I lead."

There were several factors Aaron tried to take in at once. "You mean you swore never to make another vampire." Trying to wrap his brain around the fact that Taylor wanted to include him in all of this was considerably difficult. He'd assumed Taylor had brought him along as simply a means of survival.

"But to do so would jeopardize your safety, and that is something I don't think I can risk, Aaron. No matter how badly I want to."

"Why would it jeopardize my safety?"

Because the others will see you only as food. They will consider my judgment clouded by my emotions, and you would be tortured and destroyed. I would be punished, if not destroyed myself. They do not tolerate the breaking of any oath."

"Doesn't anybody in this brotherhood create others?" No longer sure exactly what he'd gotten himself into, Aaron had already figured that it wasn't likely that any of the others would let him go free with the knowledge he had.

"No. We are it—the elite." Taylor stood and went to the dresser. Turning, he leaned back and crossed his arms, gaze steady. "I've come to want you more than is safe. It's gone beyond survival. I didn't want you to leave me—which is why you are my ghoul."

"I didn't plan on leaving you, Taylor. But how safe am I here? Can anybody grab me just because I'm food?"

"So long as you remain my ghoul, no. If you were to be turned..."

"Then we're both dead meat, right?" Scooting off the bed, Aaron slowly approached him. "To be honest, I really wasn't sure if you planned on having me around that long now that you're back in your own territory. I feel kind of out of place."

Taylor reached out and pulled Aaron close. "If I don't turn you, we will be fine. My blood is in your veins. That alone is enough to keep you safe while mortal."

His arms snaked around Taylor's neck as Aaron leaned against him. "I just wanted you to want me to stay, Taylor. I don't think I give a damn about the rest. As long as you don't kick me to the curb."

"Need you too much," Taylor whispered. "For much more than blood and sex, Aaron."

Aaron needed to know that, that he was far more than just a toy to Taylor. His own emotions were so hard to quell, and he'd already realized he was falling in love with Taylor. It was far more than just the fantasy he'd once envisioned. "Inside it hurts, Taylor. So much that I can't even think about life without you now."

"You don't have to." Taylor cupped Aaron's face and kissed him softly. "I'm yours," he murmured, "just as you are mine."

"Mine." Aaron whispered the word in a tone of awe as he stared at Taylor. The tips of his fingers gently brushed over the curve of Taylor's jaw, simply needing the touch and contact. Thinking of Taylor as his was something he'd really never allowed himself to do.

"All yours."

* * *

The massive circular room was filled with people. Aaron wasn't sure which ones were vampires or if any other mortals were present. There was no furniture, and the only decorations were the black stone pillars that lined the circumference of the room. Two curved staircases, near the walls about mid-center of the room, lead upward.

Aaron walked behind Taylor, refusing to be intimidated by the staring eyes in his direction. When Taylor stopped in front of a group, Aaron stepped to his side. In front of them was one of the most gorgeous men Aaron had ever seen.

"Good evening, Master Sol." Taylor's words were followed by a low bow, and he glanced over at Aaron, indicating Aaron should do the same. When they both straightened back up, Taylor stood with his hands clasped before him.

"My dear friend," the man before them purred. "How good it is you've come home." A slender, almost elegant hand was extended. Instead of shaking it, however, Taylor bent and kissed the man's knuckles. Sol lowered his hand once more. "Please..." He gestured toward curtains parting behind him, revealing a room piled with plush, blood red carpets and pillows with gold accents. "Join me."

Sol gave Aaron a single glance and what seemed to be an approving—albeit toothy—smile. Then he turned and led them up the black marble steps to the room. Sol's black hair resembled loose silk as it spilled in a straight line down his back. His heavy black robes were made of velvet, trimmed in red silk. He looked, in essence, like a king among his subjects.

Even though the other vampire appeared relatively young and therefore harmless, Aaron's gut feeling told him otherwise. He barely resisted the urge to press as close as he could to Taylor. Instead, he waited a moment for Taylor, then followed him. Behind Aaron, two other vampires stepped in line and ascended the steps as well.

As Taylor settled near his master, Aaron knelt off to the side, slightly behind him.

"Tell me, Taylor, is this one to be community property?" A dark, predatory gaze fastened on Aaron. Finding himself the subject of another drop-dead gorgeous vampire's interest, Aaron gave him a blank look. What in the hell did these people use to keep their looks? This one was comparable to an angel with his long, silvery blonde hair and gray eyes. Dressed all in white, the illusion had to be a joke.

"No." Though Aaron couldn't see Taylor's face, the vampire's tone made it crystal clear that Taylor was far from pleased. "Aaron is my ghoul." He turned and reached out. "Come."

Aaron took his hand and shifted closer to Taylor. An inward shiver was Aaron's only reaction to the tone of Taylor's voice. His expression showed nothing but a polite mask, even though he felt like cussing the angel dude out.

"Titus, Taylor has just returned to us after a long absence. Do not question him so." Though Sol spoke quietly, Titus instantly looked away from Aaron.

"I am sorry, Master," Titus muttered under his breath.

"Would you care for something to drink?" Sol asked Aaron, giving him a calculating smile.

"Yes, thank you." Aaron politely bowed his head.

Lifting one hand, Sol snapped his fingers. A servant scurried over and placed a knife in his hand. Its black blade glittered in the dim lights overhead, and the handle was made of obsidian carved in the shape of a dragon. Sol handed the blade to Titus, who seemed to take great pleasure in it as he reached for Taylor's left arm. Taylor hissed as the blade cut into his wrist, his fangs bared as he scowled at Titus.

"Please," Sol beckoned to Aaron, "drink."

Watching wide-eyed, Aaron didn't know what to say at first. The scent of Taylor's blood reached him, and a surge of hunger made Aaron groan. As he looked into each face, he realized he didn't have a choice, nor would his own need give him one. He didn't want to, but he reached for Taylor's hand and quickly drew his lover's wrist to his mouth.

Closing his eyes to block out the others, Aaron sealed his mouth tightly over the wound, drinking heavily. The whole situation humiliated Aaron, something he didn't enjoy at all. He did his best not to focus on anything other than Taylor.

Taylor's other hand slid around Aaron's, fingers resting over Aaron's pulse point. "Are you satisfied?" Taylor growled.

"Quite. You may stop, boy," Sol said.

Aaron obediently stopped and released Taylor's wrist. He didn't look at any of them. He didn't give a damn what any of them thought. While he was too angry at the humiliation, Aaron wasn't about to give any of them the satisfaction of seeing it.

"You are welcome here as long as you wish," Sol said to Taylor, paying no further attention to Aaron. "I wish to speak with you privately as well."

Tightening his jaw for a moment, Taylor nodded. "Thank you, Master."

With a gesture of Sol's hand, Titus stirred from his position to move closer to him. Sol's hand idly played over Titus' side as the vampire stretched out beside him. "I do expect that you will want to stay at least until after Blakely arrives. You'll be pleased to know that your estate has been maintained very carefully in your absence."

Remaining beside Taylor, Aaron watched Sol slip his hand beneath the waistband of Titus' loose pants. Keeping anything from showing in his expression, he could only pray this bullshit wouldn't be required, too.

"Thank you, Master," Taylor said under his breath. His gaze never strayed from Sol's face.

"Please do make yourself comfortable." At Sol's words, shadows began to creep from the corners of the small room. "I trust you have not forgotten your... abilities."

Taylor swallowed, hand tightening on the back of Aaron's neck. "No, Master."

Aaron's attempt to restrain himself became more and more difficult as each moment passed. The tension in the air had taken on a dark, ominous feel. Feeling the tighter hold Taylor had on him, his arm slid around Taylor, and Aaron narrowed his gaze on Sol. Whatever was about to happen, he wasn't going to like it one bit, and there probably wasn't a damn thing he could do about it.

Titus groaned as one of the shadows slid over his stomach, then down into his pants alongside Sol's hand. Another shadow swirled just in front of Aaron, as if waiting. Taking a deep breath, his fingers digging slightly into Aaron's skin, Taylor had no choice but to do as his Master silently commanded.

*I am sorry.*

A moment after Taylor's words whispered in Aaron's mind, the shadow crept over Aaron's thighs, caressing him as it moved higher.

# Chapter Thirty-Three

This couldn't be happening. Aaron stiffened, feeling the silky movement of the darkness creeping ever upward. In a moment's breath, Aaron's mood completely changed, and he barely stopped himself from laughing out loud. "You're kidding me, right? He plays with me and gets me off. And this proves what? He's a fucking gorgeous guy to begin with and can get me off?"

The shadows dissolved altogether, and Sol gave Aaron a cryptic smile. Then he turned his attention to Taylor, who was practically shaking. "You are dismissed." The words were clipped, the vampire's stare sharp enough to cut steel. "I will see you privately in two days' time."

Taylor stood abruptly, tugging Aaron up with him. "Yes, Master," he snapped. A large cut across his right cheek made him wince.

"Do not trifle with me, Taylor. You are already in deep enough as it is."

As the cut healed, Taylor bowed his head. "Yes, Master."

Not entirely sure what he missed, Aaron quickly followed Taylor. He didn't say a word, but his own amusement had returned to anger. The moment they were out of the main room, Taylor grabbed Aaron and summoned the shadows to take them to their room.

Aaron clung to Taylor within the dizzying sense of darkness that scattered his wits. When it faded, the room came blurrily into view.

The shadows faded, but Taylor didn't release Aaron. "I am sorry for that," he whispered.

"For what? I got the feeling he wanted me screaming and struggling." Aaron smirked at him. "I wasn't about to give him that. And you want to tell me what that cut was about, and what in the hell is really going on?"

"He was testing me, more than you. Sol is angry with me. I was the captain of his guard before I went to sleep."

"Yeah, I figured he was trying to seriously yank your chain. He's not happy you went to sleep, right?"

"To put it mildly," Taylor muttered. "The cut was nothing compared to what he's capable of."

"So that was just what? A smack on the wrist for being a bad boy?" Good lord, the more he figured out about all of this, the more ludicrous it all sounded.

"More or less. A warning, simply put. And a promise of much worse to come."

"You know, it's actually reassuring in an odd sort of way that vampires can be as childish as humans. Superior species, my ass."

For the first time in a while, Taylor actually laughed. "You have no idea."

"I doubt if Master would appreciate the non-distinction." Aaron wrapped his arms tightly around Taylor, hugging him. "It really doesn't matter, though. I'm with you through thick and thin, and even him."

"Mmm... absolutely." Taylor held him tight and let out a long, ragged breath. "Sol is...well, a royal pain in the ass. Literally."

"So I've noticed. But you're more important than he is. At least to me. I can put up with him as long as you're not taken away from me." His own feelings were too deeply entangled with Taylor, and he wasn't about to let go of him.

A hand cupped Aaron's chin and tilted his face up to meet Taylor's gaze. The vampire stroked his thumb across Aaron's bottom lip and smiled. "As you are to me."

Staring earnestly up at him, Aaron asked, "You don't think he realizes the truth between us, does he, Taylor?"

"He can't read my thoughts. It's not one of his abilities, though it is one of mine. It is another reason why my sleep angered him: he relied on me as his most trusted spy, so to speak. But no, he does not."

Relieved, Aaron relaxed against him. "Am I supposed to love you, though? How much am I supposed to behave so nobody becomes suspicious? That's the last thing I'd want."

Taylor was quiet for a moment. "Do you?" he finally asked.

"Do I what?" Aaron blinked owlishly at him.

"Do you love me?"

Tilting his head, Aaron eyed him, more puzzled than anything. "Yes, I do. I thought you already understood that, Taylor. I wouldn't be here if I didn't."

Instead of answering with words, Taylor captured Aaron's mouth in a hard, deep kiss. Taylor's hungry assault on his lips scattered Aaron's thoughts. He opened completely to him, pressing more tightly to Taylor's body as if trying to crawl inside him. Every part of him wanted to feel Taylor inside and out.

Gasping, Taylor pulled back. His fangs had descended, and his eyes were dark with hunger. "I need you. Now."

Aaron knew it. He could feel the effect of it rippling through him from Taylor's mind. Without hesitation, he unfastened his pants and shoved them down. His shoes came off, and he stepped out of the pants before getting rid of his shirt. The whole time he stared into the dark depths of Taylor's eyes, acutely aware of the strong pull Taylor had on him.

Taylor started stalking him, pushing Aaron back toward the bed without a single touch. "I want to watch you. Touch yourself, drive yourself to the edge, beg me for release."

Tumbling back onto the bed, Aaron stretched sensuously, more than happy to give Taylor exactly what he wanted. One hand trailed slowly over his bare chest, pausing to pinch one nipple then the other. His other hand lightly circled over his stomach before moving lower, rubbing the tips of his fingers over his cock. The small sensations drew a gasp from him, and his hips arched upward as his hand wrapped around his cock.

"That's it," Taylor purred, his clothes falling to the floor. He devoured Aaron with his gaze. "What do you want, Aaron? Where do you want me? Show me."

"I want you to watch me, Taylor." He never glanced away from Taylor or closed his eyes. Aaron pumped his cock until the need made his hips jerk upward to fuck his hand. Spreading his legs, he reached around, hand cupping against his ass and his fingers inching toward his hole. A soft moan came from him as he began to push them inside his ass. "God, it feels good, but not as sweet as you."

A deep growl rumbled from Taylor, and he crawled onto the end of the bed. The further up he went, the more he pushed Aaron's legs apart. "Does it now?"

He drew his legs up, keeping them open to give Taylor room. One finger probed his hole as his other hand continued its strokes. "I want you to do anything you want to me, Taylor."

"Move your hand," Taylor said. "Pull your legs up and hold them apart for me. Show me what I want."

Ever obedient, Aaron eagerly grabbed his legs and held the backs, leaving himself open to the vampire. Simply imagining what Taylor would do to him was enough to bring a soft whimper to his lips.

Hands on Aaron's ass, Taylor bent and spread Aaron more. "So sweet," he purred. Then he slid his tongue over Aaron's hole.

Aaron melted and sparks skittered through him. His hands squeezed tighter to his legs as he let out another needy whimper. "Taylor, please, do anything to me. Please."

Pointing his tongue, Taylor slowly rimmed the outside, then slid inside Aaron. *Do you want more?*

"Yes," Aaron hissed, unable to help the small buck of his hips. "I want more. More of you."

Smiling and pulling back, Taylor willed the shadows to fill Aaron, stretching him, spreading him. "So beautiful when you beg for me."

"Taylor!" Aaron cried out as he began riding the sensation expanding inside him. Taylor was the only one Aaron could accept doing this to him. He'd only bluffed his way through the shadow thing with Sol. His hard cock leaked steadily against his skin as sharper arousal took hold of him. "Need you, Taylor. Need you."

Spitting into his hand, Taylor slicked himself. As the shadows dissolved, he pushed inside, never leaving Aaron empty. Hips flush with Aaron's ass, Taylor caught Aaron's arms and pinned them to the bed. "Love you," he whispered. Then he began to move—stroking deep and slow.

"I need everything of you." Aaron begged him for it all, the arch of his body writhing beneath Taylor as the vampire filled him.

"Take everything. Give me everything."

Every sensation built on itself, straining Aaron's hips against Taylor. A low cry began in his throat then rose as Taylor brought him to that edge. The cry sharpened into Taylor's name when Aaron's orgasm flooded his mind and body.

Taylor tore away from the kiss and drove his fangs deep into Aaron's throat. He growled against Aaron's neck as his own orgasm shook them both, the vampire's hips ramming into Aaron as he continued to feed deeply.

The sudden surge jolted through Aaron, leaving his body shuddering convulsively with the blinding pleasure. Unable to speak, Aaron could only cling tightly to Taylor until he became too weak to hold on any longer. Even though he really didn't know what Taylor was doing, Aaron didn't try to stop him or struggle against him.

Taylor licked the wounds and bit his own wrist. Pressing it to Aaron's lips, Taylor whispered a soft prayer, something about getting out before Sol knew he'd stolen one of the formulas. Aaron barely took in that information, the world hazy. What had Taylor done?

"Drink for me, love. Come back to me, Aaron. Please."

It finally sank in, what Taylor was doing. Aaron tried to shake his head and form the words, but they wouldn't come out. It would cost Taylor too much to do this, and Aaron knew it. His mouth opened to speak, but he could make no more than a small sound.

"Shh, it's too late now. Drink, Aaron. Please. Don't leave me."

Aaron already knew he would die if he didn't, yet still he hesitated for that one moment. If he could have cried, he would have. He really didn't want to die, didn't want to leave Taylor. His throat worked as he tried to swallow the caustic liquid Taylor spilled on his tongue.

Taylor set the emptied vial aside. "Rest, love," he murmured, smoothing his fingers over Aaron's forehead. "Rest and come back to me."

Aaron's eyes closed even though he struggled against the rising darkness. It did him no good to fight it. The blackness swallowed him whole.

* * *

"See to it that everything is in order for when he wakes."

"Yes, sir." The servant nodded and left the room.

After closing the door, Taylor went to the bed and sat down. He smoothed his fingers over Aaron's brow. "Come back to me, Aaron."

A soft knock sounded on the door.

"Come in."

The door opened and a young man stepped in, closing the door behind him. "You sent for me, sir?"

"Yes." Taylor patted the bed beside Aaron. "He'll be waking soon. You've fed a new vampire, correct?"

"Yes, sir."

"Then you know it will be painful."

The donor nodded.

"Very well." Taylor smiled when there was movement beside them. He leaned over and kissed Aaron's lips softly. "Wake up, love. I'm here."

* * *

When Aaron's eyes opened, he vacantly stared into space. It took several seconds for anything to register, and the scent of blood drew a low, hungry growl from him. The sound increased in tenor as he finally looked at Taylor. Hunger rolled through his gut in tight waves of pain.

Taylor snapped his fingers. A young man moved around to the other side of the bed. Taylor helped Aaron to sit up slowly as the man slipped his shirt off. "Come on, Aaron. You're hungry. Ease it." He guided Aaron to the man's neck.

Homing in on the expanse of throat, Aaron bit hard. He couldn't yet control the hunger or the frantic draw of his lips on the fountain of blood pouring into his mouth.

Taylor let him feed until the donor's heartbeat began to slow. "Easy." He coaxed Aaron to release the donor's throat. "Aaron, you must stop now." Despite Aaron's muffled snarl, Taylor freed the donor and the wounds healed. Then he waved over the next donor.

The feeling still raged in him, demanding to be sated. Aaron watched the blond with a fierce intent. Once the guy was close enough, Aaron took hold of him, pulled him closer, and began to feed from him. The donor hissed with the untutored bite.

*Listen for the heartbeat. Follow its rhythm, Aaron. When it begins to slow, you must stop.*

Hearing the instructions in his mind, Aaron attempted to focus his senses on the man he fed from. He could hear the steady thump of the heart as he drank. It wasn't long before the pause between each beat slowed. Unfortunately, Aaron wasn't yet ready to give up his prize, and he struggled to follow Taylor's order.

"Aaron. Stop," Taylor ordered. He exerted a bit of his own power, and it washed over Aaron.

With a low growl, Aaron reluctantly released the donor. The hunger wasn't as bad as it had been initially, but he could still feel the pangs of need. Glancing between Taylor and the one he hadn't drank from yet, Aaron waited.

Taylor motioned for the third donor. "Easy now. Remember the heartbeat."

The donor sat and bared his neck to Aaron, giving him a comforting smile. He was older than the other two, as the few strands of gray in his dark brown hair showed. "Take your time," he said.

Aaron took a moment to try to compose himself. He glanced at Taylor, drawing on him in ways Aaron couldn't define. It relaxed him considerably, and he was able to at least mentally function even with the low nag of hunger that tugged at him. He leaned in, lips nuzzling against the skin before he bit down. This time the bite was far more controlled and relatively painless.

The man's arm encircled Aaron's waist, encouraging Aaron to take his time. "He's learning."

"That he is," Taylor said, stroking Aaron's hair.

"How did you find him, Taylor?"

"Long story, old friend. He found me, truth be told."

This time Aaron paid very careful attention to the sound of the heart. Finally, he completely stopped. Straightening, he smiled at Taylor. The feelings in his body had eased considerably, and finally Aaron could focus on everything else instead of the immediate desire for blood.

"You'll have to tell me the story someday." The donor released Aaron and stood up. "The car should be ready to take you to Italy in another hour. It will give you both time to talk." The other two men followed him out the door.

When they were alone, Taylor held out a hand to Aaron. "How are you feeling?"

"Weird." Aaron laughed as he grabbed Taylor's hand and tugged him down to sit on the bed. "I can smell you. Where are we?"

"We're in Paris. We have to leave for Rome, Aaron."

"I'll go anywhere you do, Taylor. Do we have to worry about Sol?" Scooting to get closer to Taylor, Aaron practically ended up in his lap.

Taylor lay back, leaving Aaron to straddle him. "I pray the Romanorum will grant me amnesty and provide sanctuary for us."

Though he probably should worry, Aaron just couldn't concentrate on the matter enough to do so. Not with the firm feel of Taylor's body beneath him. His legs tightened against Taylor's hips. "I do love you, Taylor. I wasn't sure about you changing me at first, but now I'm glad you did. I want to be around for a very long time with you."

* * *

Taylor didn't know how he'd be received within the halls of the Romanorum. He'd given up his rogue ways, but it wasn't a guarantee. Still, he had to try. He had Aaron now to think about. Taylor studied the sleeping young vampire. When he went to sleep, it was to escape the hell of the Brotherhood, the constant strive for greatness. He can't remember why he woke, only that he'd been ravenously hungry and gave little thought to how the world might have changed. Killing was a hard habit to break, and for some reason, this young man sleeping beside him had changed centuries of that same habit in just a few short days.

Aaron stirred and Taylor bent to kiss him awake. "Hey," he said, smiling against Taylor's lips.

"We have to go. Our ride will be here soon."

Aaron stretched, teasing Taylor with deliciously bare skin. Taylor wanted to simply sink himself deep inside his lover until nothing else existed. Now, however, was not the time. Taylor got out of bed before temptation won. He dressed and tossed Aaron's clothes onto the bed, not missing the knowing smile Aaron gave him.

"Don't know if it's your blood in me or what," Aaron said as he sat up and crawled across the bed to where Taylor stood by the edge. "But you can't hide from me."

"Not trying to hide," Taylor murmured. "Trying to get us moving before I give in and have my way with you again."

"Just promise me you'll do it when we get to wherever we're going, and I'll be good."

Taylor fisted a hand in Aaron's hair, earning himself a breathy gasp from his young lover. "I swear it."

A knock sounded on the door, barely there. Taylor went over and opened it while Aaron dressed. The servant bowed and handed Taylor a slip of folded paper, then left. Taylor closed the door and opened the note.

*You are to report directly to me when you arrive in Rome. Speak to no one else.*

Written in a sweeping flourish, it was signed by the one man who brought them all into existence, the one Taylor would swear allegiance to now: Diocourides.

"Taylor? What is it?"

Taylor held up the note. "A summons from Dio himself."

"Is that good? I mean, we were going there, right?"

"It's more than good. It means we won't die trying to meet with him. It means..." Taylor smiled slowly. "It means we are home."

## ABOUT THE AUTHORS
Shayne:
She writes, she makes shiny things.


Mychael:
Alter ego of Katherine Cook, Mychael focuses on gay erotic romance stories in many genres. He lives in the eastern US with his family.
https://www.mychaelblack.com
https://www.facebook.com/mblackauthor/